THE THIRTE
GRE

Also in Fontana

The Fontana Book of Great Ghost Stories
The 2nd Fontana Book of Great Ghost Stories
The 3rd Fontana Book of Great Ghost Stories
The 4th Fontana Book of Great Ghost Stories
The 5th Fontana Book of Great Ghost Stories
The 6th Fontana Book of Great Ghost Stories
The 7th Fontana Book of Great Ghost Stories
Ed. Robert Aickman

The 9th Fontana Book of Great Ghost Stories
The 10th Fontana Book of Great Ghost Stories
The 11th Fontana Book of Great Ghost Stories
Ed. R. Chetwynd-Hayes

Tales of Fear and Fantasy
The Night Ghouls
R. Chetwynd-Hayes

Lord Halifax's Ghost Book
Lord Halifax

Frighteners
Frighteners 2
Ed. Mary Danby

The Thirteenth Fontana Book of Great

Ghost Stories

Selected by R. Chetwynd-Hayes

Collins/Fontana

First published by Fontana Books 1977

Made and printed in Great Britain by
William Collins Sons & Co Ltd Glasgow

CONTENTS

ACKNOWLEDGEMENTS

The editor gratefully acknowledges permission to reprint copyright material to the following:

Mr Denis Wheatley and Hutchinson Ltd for THE CASE OF THE LONG-DEAD LORD from *Gunmen, Gallants and Ghosts.*

The author for THE LONELY APPARITION, © Charles Thornton 1977.

The author for CRIMSON LAKE, © Daphne Froome 1977.

The author for OLD SHADOWS by Ken Alden, © Ken Alden 1977.

The author and Harvey Unna Ltd for THE MAN WITH THE FLUTE by Rosemary Timperley, © Rosemary Timperley 1977.

The Estate of the late W. Somerset Maugham and William Heinemann Ltd for THE TAIPAN by W. Somerset Maugham.

The author for INTO THE MAD, MAD WORLD by Terry Tapp, © Terry Tapp 1977

The author for DISAPPEARANCE by Roger Malisson, © Roger Malisson 1977

The author for THE GHOST MACHINE by Roger F. Dunkley, © Roger F. Dunkley 1977.

Mrs Berta Oliver for THE ROCKER by Oliver Onions, from *Widdershins.*

The author for THE CAPE COD POLTERGEIST by Margaret Chilvers Cooper, © Margaret Chilvers Cooper 1977.

The author for 28 TOWER STREET by Duncan Forbes, © Duncan Forbes 1977.

The author and Michael Bakewell Associates Ltd for MOTHER LOVE by Pamela Cleaver, © Pamela Cleaver 1977.

The author and London Management for MY DEAR WIFE by R. Chetwynd-Hayes, © R. Chetwynd-Hayes 1977.

EDITOR'S NOTE

Every effort has been made to trace the owners of the copyright material in this book. It is the Editor's belief that the necessary permissions from publishers, authors and authorized agents have been obtained, but in the case of any question arising as to the use of any material, the Editor, while expressing regret for any errors, will be pleased to make the necessary corrections in future editions of the book.

INTRODUCTION

I wonder why we all – and I do mean all – are so interested in ghosts? Maybe it is a subconscious need to have some confirmation that there is an afterlife; that we continue to exist, in no matter what form, once this brief earthly journey comes to an end. Undoubtedly there would be certain advantages in being a ghost. One could – given freedom of movement – sit in on Cabinet meetings, take a free trip round the world and scare the living daylights out of anyone one did not like.

But of course ghosts rarely do have freedom of movement. Like Murdock Glourie in *The Ghost Goes West* the disembodied spirit is usually doomed to walk a predestined haunting path, over a period that can stretch into many centuries.

Such was the fate of the ghost in *The Case of the Long-Dead Lord* by Denis Wheatley. I, for many years, have bowed my head in respectful admiration of Mr Wheatley's brilliant imagination and devoutly wished I could imitate his mind-engrossing style. Those of you who have read *Strange Conflict* must have tried – at least once – to practise continuity and recapture memories of your adventures on the astral plane during sleeping hours. Once I was partially successful. Having read the book for the umpteenth time, I retired to bed, determined to find out if there was anything in the theory or not. Suddenly I found myself staring down at my own sleeping body. I was so frightened, I instantly woke up drenched in perspiration, my heart thumping like an overworked steam-engine. All right – it may have been no more than a vivid dream, but it certainly seemed to be very real.

Having created a psychic detective of my own, I was delighted to meet Mr Wheatley's Neils Orsen, and a very able investigator he is too. How nice it would be if he and my fellow could work together one day.

The Lonely Apparition by Charles Thornton is short – a mere cold breath of a story – but I accepted it because of the visual impact, the stark reality that peeps out from behind the fabric of make-believe. Look upon it as a chilling tit-bit at a macabre feast.

The Dead Smile by F. Marion Crawford, though, is a dreadful tale, a real piece of juicy macabre. Read this:

And he went in alone and saw that the body of Sir Vernon Ockram was leaning upright against the stone wall, and that his head lay on the ground near by with the face turned up, and the dried leathern lips smiled horribly at the dried-up corpse, while the iron coffin, lined with black velvet, stood open on the floor.

And very nice too.

In contrast *Crimson Lake* by Daphne Froome is as modern as the latest pop song, and is in fact about young musicians who inherit an old theatre and run foul of the late owner. Daphne Froome is a newcomer to this genre, but I foresee a great future for her if she continues to turn out stories like this.

New ground is also broken by Ken Alden in *Old Shadows.* Looking back along the avenue of time and viewing the scene of one's childhood is usually a nostalgic experience, and we are reminded of L. P. Hartley's words: 'The past is a foreign country, they speak a different language there.' But were all the events that we accepted as mere manifestations of the commonplace exactly as they seemed? Was the maid who screamed just a hysterical girl with boy-friend trouble? And what about Nana, the large collie dog?

Think back – try to remember.

Rosemary Timperley has again created that rather sad, haunting atmosphere which makes her ghost stories so readable. In *The Man With the Flute* the narrator is a child, who relates the eerie events in a most matter-of-fact style. I like the description of the flute player:

He himself looked rather like a featherless and starved bird, shoulders hunched high, spindly legs black-outlined against the snowy road behind him.

W. Somerset Maugham is not usually associated with ghost stories, but *The Taipan* is a very good one. A taipan appears to have been 'number one in not the least important branch of the most important English firm in China'. Now – having tucked that piece of information under your belt, find out what happened to the taipan after he had seen three ghostly Chinamen digging a grave.

It gives me great pleasure to include two glorious oldies, found in some bound magazines dating back to 1886. First we have *Not Yet Solved* by that indefatigable writer – so loved by Victorians – Anonymous; then *The Grey Cottage* by Mrs Claxton. I am not going to tell you anything about the story lines (that would spoil your enjoyment), but request you read them by candlelight. Better still, read them aloud to a group of friends.

Terry Tapp is another newcomer to this series and his *Into the Mad, Mad World* is told in a most imaginative way. I have often pondered on the possibility that some so-called mad people may have a clarity of vision not granted to the reputedly sane. Take the classic example of a man who thinks he's Napoleon: well – perhaps he is. In Mr Tapp's story Rachel Bowden knows what she has seen and why she did certain things, but the *sane* people decide she is mad. The reader must decide if they are right.

Guy de Maupassant has inspired many modern writers, not least of whom is W. Somerset Maugham. *The Hostelry* is possibly one of his least known stories, which only goes to show that anthologists often do not do their homework. What could be more horrifying than this:

Aroused by the noise, the dog began to howl in terror, and ran hither and thither in the room, trying to find out whence the danger threatened. When he came to the door, he sniffed at the edge of it, and began howling, snorting, and snarling, his hair bristling, his tail erect.

A ghost trying to get in?

Roger Malisson writes the kind of story I like, having a mind that can sense the teeming world that borders our own. In *Disappearance* we have a really unique plot that only allows us – so to speak – a glimpse through a parting in the curtain on the last page.

As regular readers of this series must be aware, Roger F. Dunkley relates his ghost stories with tongue wedged firmly in his cheek, and *The Ghost Machine* has us chuckling and shivering, while marvelling at the ingenuity of the plot. When I first read this story, an idea struck me that one day – be it in a hundred or a million years – someone will invent a machine that might quite well transform our thought waves into visual images. In fact, if civilization continues, such an invention is a certainty. Think – our every action may one day provide unlimited entertainment for yet to be born generations.

Have you anything to hide?

Ever since reading *The Beckoning Fair One* I have placed Oliver Onions among the top ten ghost story writers of all time. *The Rocker* is subtle, a beautiful character study of Aunt Rachel, who rocks away in her chair while the gipsy woman speaks of the small shape she is holding in her arms.

Margaret Chilvers Cooper (as I mentioned in *The Twelfth Fontana Book of Great Ghost Stories*) lives in Falmouth, Massachusetts, USA, and again she has written a story which has its setting on the North American coastline. There is humour, a nice tight plot and some superb writing. And of course, *The Cape Cod Poltergeist.* What more can one ask for?

I am pleased to welcome Duncan Forbes to the ranks of the fear-mongers. *28 Tower Street* is a ghost story set against a modern background, written in a crisp, engrossing style, and has a lovely twist in the tail. We are also given a glimpse of university life, which I must say, appears to be very entertaining.

Mother Love by Pamela Cleaver is a beautiful little ghost story, with an exciting twist at the end. I hope I'm not giving the game away, when I quote: 'The road to hell is paved with good intentions.' Mothers have always been a nuisance to men with broad-minded ideas and Miss Cleaver's ghostly parent is no exception.

Last of all there is my own, very humble offering. I like to think that *My Dear Wife* is a story with a moral: always make sure you have got rid of one love before taking on a new one. Otherwise life – and death – can become very complicated.

Well – there we are. Eighteen stories. Eighteen authors – ancient and modern – who are prepared to guide you along the misty road that terminates in the land of what may well be. I can only wish you an exciting, if not a particularly comfortable journey.

R. CHETWYND-HAYES

THE CASE OF THE LONG-DEAD LORD

Denis Wheatley

'Thank God you've come,' Bruce Hemmingway cried, as he gripped the hand of the little man for whom he'd been waiting on the platform at Inverness.

'Your wire interested me,' Neils Orsen replied with a gentle smile. 'What's this about my being a naturalist?'

'I'll tell you in a minute. Let's go over to the hotel.'

As the two men walked across the street they made an oddly assorted couple. Neils Orsen was small and lightly built, with transparently pale skin and large, luminous blue eyes. His domed head with a high intelligent brow and mass of soft fair hair appeared too large for his diminutive body. Hatless, dressed in pale grey, carrying a basket conspicuously labelled 'Live Cat', he made a striking contrast to the tall, dark-haired American by his side.

Over coffee in the hotel Bruce explained while the Siamese cat, Păst, sat on a chair beside them, lapping cream.

'Arkon Clyde, a friend of mine from back home, has taken Castle Stuart for the shooting. I drew up the lease and as the Clydes have never been in Scotland before they asked me to see them settled in. At the moment there's just the old man, who is completely absorbed in books, and his glamorous daughter Fiona; their guests don't arrive for about a week. I've known the girl for some time; she's typical of her generation; sensible, a bit hard-boiled, but full of fun. Yet, when I arrived two days after them, I found her all shot to pieces.

'Well, that puzzled me quite a bit, but the only thing I could get out of her was that for the first time in her life she was suffering from the most appalling nightmares.

'The day before yesterday I took her a walk to explore the ruins of the old castle which are some two miles away. Leading to it there's a lovely avenue of old beeches. We'd only got half-way along it when suddenly she stopped dead, and a queer look came into her eyes. "I've been here before," she whispered to herself, then she began to mutter in what seemed to me like Gaelic. I took hold of her hands and shook her and she looked at me with wide, blinded eyes. As I called her name the spell seemed to snap. She just said she was tired of walking and wanted to go back.

'Maybe I'm wrong, but it didn't seem to me a case for an ordinary doctor, so I asked Arkon if I might have a friend of mine who was a naturalist to stay for a few days, because I didn't want them to know you are a ghost-hunter, and wired you that night.'

'Has anything happened since?' the little Swede asked in his careful English that held hardly a trace of accent.

'No, nothing; except that she never goes into her room if she can help it and spends most of her time wandering alone round the grounds.'

'Does she strike you as an imaginative young woman?'

'Far from it. She has brains as well as looks and graduated in Law at Columbus.'

Neils leaned back, placing the tips of his fingers together.

'So she doesn't like her room? Have you been into it?'

'Yes; I even spent the night before last there, but I slept like a top and yesterday she insisted on returning to it. I can't understand it – I'm sure she's terrified of it and yet she refuses to move.'

'The girl may be abnormally psychic; as neither you nor, apparently, her father are in the least disturbed.'

'Oh, one thing I forgot. She said that her door wouldn't stay shut. Well, the night I spent there it didn't budge an inch. I know, because I fixed a piece of cotton over the opening and it wasn't broken in the morning.'

'At certain phases of the moon, perhaps,' Neils hazarded, 'the Force – if there is a Force – might be stronger.'

'Maybe. But she didn't sleep any better in my room. It's killing her, Neils. A few days ago she was at least scared, and fighting it. Now she's just vague and won't talk. She looked like death at breakfast this morning, but of course her father didn't notice anything; he was buried in some book or other. I don't like leaving her alone. If only I could get that dog to stay with her.'

'What dog?'

'The boar-hound that belongs to the place. He liked her at first, but now he runs away as soon as she appears. Can people be possessed, Neils?'

'Certainly; but we've hardly enough evidence to pre-suppose such a thing in this case. Miss Clyde sounds like a girl suffering from a species of nervous collapse. Of course, a place having the history of Castle Stuart behind it would be filled with vibrations from the past, but apart from the dog's behaviour there is nothing to suggest that her condition is the result of psychic causes.'

'I know, Neils. But I'll swear something queer is going on. Ten days ago, in London, Fiona was a normal, healthy girl with bags of energy; now she's a nervous wreck and so washed out that one might – yes, one might even think that a vampire was sapping her vitality.'

Pāst closed his eyes and purred softly. 'Let us go,' said Neils, 'to Castle Stuart.'

As Bruce turned the car into the gateway the sun was brilliant over the Firth and mountain heads, and he felt a little ashamed at having summoned the famous psychic investigator for so nebulous a purpose. The Castle looked a mild architectural curiosity, but no more. There was nothing sinister here where the drive wound among the sun-burnished scrub and pines; Neils, with the cat upon his knees, glanced up at the brown stone battlements.

'But this is not very old,' he said, smiling.

'Oh, no, only about a hundred and fifty years. It's just a copy. The ruins of the original castle are about two miles away. It marks one boundary of the estate.'

In the great hall sunlight stabbed the worn surfaces of ancient flags that hung motionless, drooping long, twisted shadows across the stairway. While the servants were taking up Orsen's luggage the Swede stood very still, his head inclined as though he listened. Bruce had left him, to look for Fiona. He brought her through the garden door into the hall, where she stood, bathed in the dusty sunlight, her golden hair responding to its caresses; but her lovely green eyes were cold and distant as she shook hands with Orsen.

Her father rushed upon them from the library, American hospitality in every gesture. He was delighted to welcome Bruce's friend . . . Pāst was cute . . . He had found some interesting material on the bird-life of the island . . . and the books were ready beside the sherry for the attention of Mr Orsen.

But Neils refused the wine, and Bruce said sadly, 'I'm afraid he never touches alcohol.'

Throughout luncheon Neils contrived to show a surprising knowledge of his purported subject and Arkon Clyde took to him immediately; but Fiona obviously found it an effort to concentrate her attention sufficiently to appear barely civil, and directly the meal was over she excused herself abruptly.

''Fraid my girl doesn't take to this sort of life very easily,' Clyde said in apology as the door closed behind her. 'I guess she finds it a bit dull after New York.'

'I'll go and see if I can amuse her,' Bruce volunteered. Neils made no sign. His small, gnome-like figure remained bowed in contemplation; one hand was playing with a lock of hair.

Bruce found Fiona curled up on a garden seat behind the Castle. Sitting down, he said earnestly: 'Fiona, do tell me what's wrong. It's sticking out a mile that you've got something on your mind.'

'No! If I tell, you'll say I'm crazy.' She turned away from him and he saw the scarlet mouth tremble. 'I'm beginning to think I must be; no sane person could feel the way I do – could –' she spoke in a hard, strained voice – 'could feel *haunted*!'

As he remained silent she went on desperately: 'Dammit, Bruce, the Castle *is* haunted, and you know it. Why did you let Father bring me here?'

Bruce nodded. 'So I was right! Now listen, Fiona. My friend, Neils Orsen, is not really a naturalist but the world's greatest psychic investigator. I wired for him when I saw how things were with you, and I'm darned glad I did, because if anyone can help you, he can. Let me fetch him; then you can tell him all about it.'

'I don't think anyone can help me, but you can get him if you promise that Father shan't be worried about me.'

When Bruce returned with Orsen, she was sitting in the same position, staring at the ground. She turned her head slightly as they sat down. 'Give me a cigarette, please, Bruce.' Her hand shook as she held it. 'There's something after me in this place,' she began. 'It won't let me alone. I felt odd when I first saw the Castle as we came up the drive. I knew just how it would look. That gave me a kind of shock, and I didn't tell Father, but I wanted to run away. I knew I oughtn't to go in or stay here. I lost the feeling a little until the evening – I was busy unpacking and getting the place straight. Then, when I was alone in my room before dinner, the door swung open suddenly and made me jump. It was perfectly light, and I could see nothing, but I was scared and ran out of the room. That damned door's been opening every night – except when Bruce slept there – and there's a queer, cold feeling in my head, as though I were forgetting how to think. All the time I have the idea that I know this place – that something is going to happen to me again. If only I could remember what – I might prevent it; but I can't. Wherever I go the air is full of whispers that I can't quite hear – and that was all – until last night.'

'Last night,' Bruce repeated.

She nodded. 'Yes; I was so frightened and wretched that I decided to sleep downstairs. I waited until you and Father were in your rooms. I thought perhaps the boar-hound would be sleeping in the hall; so I stood at the head of the stairs and whistled to him. And from my room – I'd left the door open – there came the most horrible chuckle, very hoarse and – and liquid. The Thing was there – it was watching me – laughing at me. I could feel it.'

'What did you do?' Orsen said quietly.

'I heard the dog growl and I ran down to him – but he was scared of something and wouldn't come near me. I stayed in the hall till about four o'clock. I couldn't sit still and I couldn't sleep, so when the light came I went for a walk. I got back about seven, had a bath and came down to breakfast. Oh, God! I'm frightened, Bruce – and I've never been frightened before. It'll get me and keep me for ever and ever. Don't let it! For God's sake don't let it!' She began to sob hysterically.

Neils stroked her hand soothingly. 'I'll do my very best to help you, I promise. Meanwhile, I suggest that you come and lie down in the hall. You have nothing to fear for the moment and you might be able to get some sleep.'

When they had made her comfortable Bruce offered to show Orsen his room. The man-servant had unpacked all the suit-cases save one. 'I kept the key,' Neils smiled, 'and I'll see to it later. It contains my cameras.'

Bruce had already seen the cameras in Orsen's company on one strange adventure, but their process – Orsen's invention – was a mystery to him. Neils explained them only by saying that their plates were abnormally sensitive. He said the same thing of his sound-recorder, an instrument like a miniature dictaphone. Bruce wondered what his friend thought of Fiona's story but knew from past experience that he would have to wait until the little man chose to enlighten him.

'Where is Miss Clyde's room?' Orsen was asking.

'Across the passage, the second door; I'll sleep in it again if you like.'

Neils shook his head. 'No, Păst and I will occupy it tonight.'

He strayed towards the window and looked out across the Firth to where the blue hills melted into the horizon. 'What a history those moors could tell,' he said thoughtfully. 'Can you hear the skirl of pipes, Bruce, or see the kilted ghosts marching up across the heather?'

'No,' said Bruce uncomfortably. 'All the same, I'm jolly glad I asked you to come up here. I'll leave you now, as I expect you'd like to get your things straight.' Bruce was a normal practical person, but as he left his small friend, standing with arms folded, heavy head sunk forward, and eyes half-closed, he thought – Neils himself gives me the creeps at times.

Fiona was no longer in the hall, and going outside he found her lying on the grass at the entrance to the wild garden. As he approached she sat up and said coldly: 'By the way, your friend is not thinking of spending the night in my room, is he?'

'He certainly is.'

'Well, he won't find anything. Tell him not to fuss.' She stretched her arms above her head. '*I'm* not worrying any more; I feel too tired to care.'

Bruce stared at her. He could hardly believe that this calm aloof creature had been sobbing hysterically on his shoulder half an hour before. 'Fiona,' he pleaded, 'there's one thing you must promise. Stick by me and Neils. We won't let any harm come to you.'

She smiled queerly. 'I think the harm has come to me already, and I'm living with it. Let me alone, Bruce; I'm not frightened any more.' She turned away from him towards the house; but half an hour later through sheer inertia she had consented to move into the other wing of the Castle for the coming night.

'Everything is ready,' Neils said to Bruce after dinner. 'I have the cameras fixed and I've taken other precautions.' He ran his fingers through his hair. 'By the way, where's the girl?'

'She's in the music-room; I'll go to her, I think.'

'Let me. Without her knowing it I may be able to strengthen her sub-conscious defences so that she gets some sleep. You go into the library and talk to Mr Clyde.' Neils was gone as quietly as a shadow.

On their way to bed he halted Bruce at the door of his own room. 'I'll come in here with you for half an hour in case the servants are about.' He shut the door and drew back the window curtains. Pāst watched him with colourless, unblinking eyes as he added quietly: 'There *is* something here.'

'What d'you think it is?'

'I can't say for certain. There are earth-bound spirits which can do great harm. You've heard me talk of such things before – of the dark places where those who have not yet passed over must lurk, and long to return. Alternatively, although this place is not old as castles go, it may have seen bloodshed. Torture or murder done for power cause vibrations and echoes that never die. If they can find some material thing to focus on they may become evil entities of great power, and even materialize at times. I have not felt any strong evil here, but when I was with Miss Clyde tonight I needed all my strength to resist a sense of bitterness, of seeking for justice, a cold and lost feeling at the heart. Perhaps that room – ' he pointed across the passage – 'holds the secret. We shall see.'

'May I watch with you?'

'No. I want you to go to the other wing and stay beside her door until it is light.'

While the hours crept by and silence held Castle Stuart as though with a mighty hand, Bruce sat leaning his head against the lintels of Fiona's door. He had no sense of the ridiculous. At times he dozed. At times he watched the slowly gathering shadows that touched the angles of wall and stairway and crawled along the vaulted ceiling; swirling like an eddying tide around his feet. Twice the door at his cheek swung open and he heard Fiona come to shut it. Down in the well of the hall he heard the boar-hound whining in its sleep, but no sound of alarm came from Fiona's room and none came from the far side of the great staircase where Orsen kept vigil. By four o'clock the short northern night was over, and having seen the cold grey dawn begin to steal through the windows, Bruce sought his bed.

He slept late and found no opportunity to be alone with Neils until Clyde retired into the library and Fiona had set out on her morning walk.

Neils looked pale and weary; his eyelids drooped. 'There was nothing,' he said, 'nothing at all. And you?'

'Nothing. Her door opened twice, but she didn't look out.'

'Did she open it?'

'I don't know. I heard her come and shut it, but this morning when I asked her how she had slept she didn't complain of anything.'

'I have never passed a night in a room so free of vibrations,' the Swede said slowly. 'It is most perplexing. Pāst, too, felt nothing or he would certainly have shown it; and he is perhaps the severest of all tests. I think,' he added, 'I will spend tonight down in the hall.'

They passed an uneasy day and were glad when Fiona and her father retired to bed.

Again Bruce kept watch. Again, save for the opening and shutting of the door, he was not disturbed, and in the morning Neils, too, reported an untroubled night.

Fiona had now become so far withdrawn from the three men that, to Bruce's mind at least, she seemed to move among them like a spirit. She did not appear unhappy, but her wide green eyes were heavy and shadowed, contrasting violently with the transparent pallor of her face, and her lovely hair seemed to reflect the moon rather than the sun. She made polite conversation at meals, and escaped after them. Every effort that Bruce made to talk to her was coldly received.

At dinner on the third evening Neils spoke only when addressed. For the rest of the time he was silent, his gaze fixed on Fiona. She had not changed from the tweeds she had worn all day and sat calm and composed, her eyes staring vacantly at the table.

'Only six days to the twelfth,' Clyde said. 'I hope I shall have the pleasure of Bruce's company and yours, Mr Orsen, for the first few days at least.'

'Not mine, I fear,' Orsen said absently.

'But you won't be leaving us so soon?'

'Tomorrow, I'm afraid.'

Bruce checked his astonishment. By no look, by no lift of the eyebrow or whispered word had Neils given him a hint. Fiona heard of Orsen's projected departure without speaking. She ate practically nothing. Before coffee was served she got abruptly to her feet and left the room. Her father stared after her with a worried frown creasing his forehead.

'I think Fiona must have gone *fey*,' he said, 'she looks mighty queer tonight.'

Orsen glanced quickly at his host. 'Why should she go *fey*? Only Scottish people are supposed to do that.'

'Well, she is Scotch – or anyway, a good half. Her mother was a McAin.'

Bruce saw that Orsen's enormous eyes were gleaming with suppressed excitement. But it was not until they had left the table and were alone that he whispered urgently:

'Her Scottish ancestry! I felt just now we should learn something important tonight. Quick! We must hunt the library for any books dealing with the history of Castle Stuart.'

For an hour the two men searched, dragging out volume after volume and frantically scanning their pages for a clue; they had almost despaired, when suddenly Orsen gave a cry of relief.

'This – this should give us the link we seek. It's the history of Castle Stuart, translated into English by the Reverend Father Cox, Chaplain to the Castle from 1698 to 1717.' He ran his finger down the index and turning to a page half-way through the book, began to read:

'*Of all the Lordes of Castle Stuart, they do tell that Donald Stuart was the blackest of them all. He were fitter companie for men-at-arms in their drunken brawls than for the fair young maide he did bring to be his bryde.*

'*She was the Ladie Fiona McAin, own daughter to the McAin of Crath, a winsome lass of sixteen summers who did grieve most sorely to leave her mother's side.*'

'Good God!' Bruce broke in. 'D'you realize Fiona's mother was a McAin and there's the extraordinary coincidence of the Christian names?'

'Of course,' Orsen nodded impatiently. 'It's something of this kind that I've been hunting for.' And he read on:

'It becometh us not to linger on that mating, for of a truth it was of an eagle and a dove, contrarie to the laws of nature and a thing offensive in the eyes of God. Poor maide how could she find happiness with such a spouse, and who shall caste blame upon her that she did welcome the young Lorde Ninan when fresh from the Court of France and full of the gracies of the French he did come as a guest for a while beneath Black Donald's roof?

'Lorde Ninan was a courtly, slender man, with smiling face and witty tongue. He did strum upon the lute for the Ladie Fiona's pleasure, write poesie for her and in the French fashion oft did kiss her hand.

'Some say that no more passed between the twain than this, for well did the Ladie Fiona know the jealous heart of her own dark Lorde. Yet on a night of feasting – so the tale is told – when the women had withdrawn and the men were in their cups, Black Donald did suddenlie miss the Lorde Ninan from his board and calling for his claymore he did stagger up the stairs to his Ladie's chamber.

'The lovers herde his loud approach, and knowing there to be murder in his drunken vengeful heart, the Ladie Fiona took Lorde Ninan's hande and guided him by a secret stair behind the tapestry down to the inner court.

'But Black Donald knew well the secret stair, and swift for all the liquor he had drunk, followed cursing upon their heels.

'They had but reached the postern gate when he espied them and shouting to his men-at-arms rushed after. Near-by the well Lorde Ninan turned at bay, but the Stuart clansmen fell upon him piercing him with a dozen pikes and skean dhus, so that he fell backwards over the well's rim, saving himself from plunging into its rockie depths onlie by the clutch of one stronge hand.

'The Ladie Fiona screamed for them to spare him but he knew his life was done, and as he hung there he cried aloud:

' "Fiona! I'll wait for thee, m'darling!" Then with one stroke did Black Donald slice off the clutching hande and the young Lorde fell to his death in the icie water sixty feet below.

' 'Tis said that the Lorde Ninan's spirit doth wait there, uneasy stille, so that in passing the end of the avenue that

leads up to that grim stronghold, the belated traveller yet may hear the last laugh of Black Donald when his bloodie wille was done, and that last heart-crye of the Lorde Ninan:

'*"Fiona! I'll wait for thee, m'darling – I'll wait for thee."*'

Orsen closed the book and stood up. 'The whole thing is clear now. It may be a case of re-incarnation or merely the McAin strain in Fiona's blood coupled with her given name. The restless spirit of Lord Ninan still waits for his love to join him. This world is a misty, timeless place to earth-bound spirits and that of Lord Ninan cannot distinguish between our Fiona and the Fiona who lived three hundred years ago; but it has become vaguely aware of her presence in the neighbourhood and is using all the power it can command to draw her to it.'

'Then her father must be told at once,' Bruce said quickly, 'and arrangements made for her to leave Scotland for good tomorrow.'

Neils nodded. 'Yes. It is she who is haunted; not the Castle or her room. That is why no manifestation occurs when she is not present. She must be got away as soon as possible, and in the meantime it's most important that she should not be allowed to go anywhere near the old ruin. The gravest possible danger awaits her there. If she were drawn to the place it's a virtual certainty that her mental resistance would be overcome and she'd feel herself compelled to throw herself down that well.'

'Right,' said Bruce. 'I'll go and tell her that you've found the root of the trouble and warn her not to leave the house.' He turned abruptly as Clyde came into the room, saying with a worried look:

'Bruce, I'm anxious about Fiona. The servants tell me she went out half an hour ago. She didn't even take a coat and it gets damp at this time of night. I wish you'd go and . . .'

Before he had time to complete his sentence Bruce leaped for the door and they heard his footsteps thunder across the hall.

Clyde had glimpsed the look of horror in Bruce's eyes and now he saw the strained expression on Orsen's face.

'What's this,' he exclaimed. 'What's happened?'

'We can only pray,' Orsen said quietly. 'Bruce can run faster than we can. Please God he will be in time.'

Up the rough track with the queer grey sky overhead and the lone moors hunched and darkening on either side, Bruce ran like a man possessed. A mist had risen off the sea; rags and rafes of it danced on the air. Here and there it came down solidly. He stumbled and fell over a tuft of heather. And now the mist came more shrouding and more white. A curlew sobbed its cry somewhere in the silence, and the trees at the roadside reared their great arms heavenwards in mockery.

He ran on, his breath coming in short gasps, knowing nothing but the blind necessity to be in time. As he topped the rise above the old castle, something told him he was too late. Down into the eerie mist he plunged and instantly felt a chill, as if a cold hand grasped his throat. He fell again, staggered to his feet, and ran on desperately across the turf. His footsteps dragged as though he was wading through a bog. A cold whiteness was all about him and with its physical desolation there bore upon his brain another darkness – a sense of evil, too sickening to be borne. He was crouched and groping. He muttered a prayer that died in his throat. Out of the gloom the stones reared, spectral and forbidding. 'Fiona!' he shouted. 'Fiona!'

The swathes of fog beat at his face. 'Fiona!' he called again. 'For God's sake answer.'

Cold, he thought suddenly. Cold – cold – cold. A faint wind whispered through the ruins. He passed his hand across his forehead. He did not know what thoughts they were which seized his brain and cramped it until no feeling came to him but one of intense fear. The wind whispered louder. Now he was up again and running forward. The evil mist was throttling him, but ahead he saw the figure of a girl – a girl who stayed at the edge of a dark, yawning pit. The mist had become a solid wall blocking his way; the wind rose to a shrill scream. He shut his eyes.

'Oh, Lord God, help me because –' strangely inspired the words came to his lips – 'because there is none other that fighteth for us but only Thou, Oh God.' Then the mist was rent as though two great hands had torn it asunder and he was at Fiona's side, dragging her back. He felt her body fall limply against him; and now where the dark pit had gaped there was only the shallow, rock-filled ruin of an old well.

Lifting his head he saw that the mist had gone. Cool and grey under the evening sky lay the stones of old Castle Stuart. He stood there for a time holding Fiona in his arms. She stirred and smiled at him:

'What happened, Bruce . . . Why are we here? . . . He called me . . . Why did he call me so urgently? . . . Why did he want me?'

'He's gone.'

'Did you send him away?' she asked faintly. 'Thank you, Bruce.'

'I think,' he said, 'we should thank Neils Orsen.'

THE LONELY APPARITION

Charles Thornton

There was nothing golden about the autumn dusk of Wandsworth, and the old tenement that had withstood a hundred seasons was now withstanding drizzle – cold and incessant. A solitary tree in its forecourt that stretched naked branches to claw at the clouds went unnoticed by the orderly file of umbrella-topped shapes as they disappeared into the basement.

At a vantage point across the road where traffic tyres hissed, stood another shape – a woman. If mortal eyes could see, the image was tall and elegant. Her hair was grey and shingled into tight small waves, clearly a style of the past. She had been ordered to wait – to search – but not to torment or coax.

Her endless vigil had taken her to Mayfair, to Chelsea, then Belgravia and back. Down to the river and the houses alongside. Through the portals of palaces and the thresholds of slums, ever hoping, ever yearning for a glimpse or a meeting but above all – a call. Now it was here at Wandsworth that she watched.

The dusk had crept into the darkness and the rain, progressing from drizzle, began to hit the pavement like iced spears. The umbrellaed file was diminishing fast. It was time that she joined them.

Through a cab, then a bus, now a jaywalking boy, her shape glided and hovered at the shoulder of the last entrant. The door closed and the pungent smell of incense raked the atmosphere, then became thicker in a lounge heavily draped and almost void of light. Arrowheads of flame were poised motionless on candles as the expectant group took their places around a glass-topped table. The woman looked at them all intensely. There was not a sign of the face she sought and yet this time – perhaps this once – she would wait. She had witnessed immortal miracles and she felt she was due for one.

A frail crone with a face drained colourless into skull-like proportions sat in a high-backed chair. She peered at the group seated before her. Then the silence was cracked and the voice was a wheeze.

'Link your hands – concentrate.'

That voice – the woman had heard it before. Her memory spanned the years. It clamped tightly on the time – the place. A room in Mayfair – a young girl crying – the voice of her dead husband pleading for her to join him – the suicide and the exposure of a fraudulent medium who took without remorse a substantial donation left in the will of the young girl. It was twenty years ago, but mortal memory is short. The gathering, unsuspecting and gullible, merely sat and obeyed. Their infantile response incensed the woman. Now she must act – but how?

She had been, unlike others, reduced to an invisible spectre: a condition of her acceptance on the other side. But here was her chance to do good. To put paid, once and for all, to the menace at the table. As the medium wheezed again the woman's vibrations searched for help.

A thin haze of smoke began to drift across the heads of the group. It was part of the reply in response to a bogus spiritual call from the swaying figure at the head of the table. This was followed by a voice – an echoing voice of a young man. The woman – the invisible ghost – knew that the controls were under the ledge of the table, at the fingertips of the medium. She saw a young woman's tears well at the sound of the voice, and heard her high-pitched cry of recognition.

'Oh, Peter – darling Peter.'

She was easy meat. A distorted tape-recording had seen to that, and the victim was in a believing mood. The voice from the tape grated on.

'Clare – Clare. I am lonely. It is grey here without you. Join me. Join me . . .'

The plea whined and faded and the apparition, moving with a whisper of annoyance, disturbed the flame on the candles. Their sudden dancing from the eerie wind caused shadows to fall and rise across the room. The medium stopped swaying and looked first at the group then, grimacing, towards the window. She mumbled a word of apology as she rose from her chair, and moved towards a heavy drape. The muffle of traffic nudging its way through the rain broke the silence, and the old woman annoyingly pulled the drape aside and looked at the tightly shut pane. The ghostly observer was losing patience.

All through her ageless vigil she had obeyed her calling. But now, for the good of all, and at the risk of dreaded consequences, she must act beyond instruction. She resolved to make her move: but at the last moment – something was happening outside.

Everyone heard the skid followed by the high squeal of brakes. The darkened room buried deep in the basement was suddenly filled with the front of a bus. Its great wheels ploughed over the medium, spraying glass, window frame and bricks in all directions. The group around the table fled in horror to the safety of the far end of the room. The bonnet of the bus rose once in its momentum, then fell and rested, ejecting the driver through the windscreen. His inert body lay face down against the wall, and somewhere beneath an oily axle an old woman died.

Stunned, the huddled group gazed at the carnage. It had revealed an old tape-recorder, dragged from its hiding place by wires still attached to a splintered table. All too clearly, the invisible one knew why this had happened. She moved away smiling thanks to someone – somewhere above her.

The rain was still pouring. She turned once and saw passengers leaving safely from the bus's rear. A covered body was being carried on a stretcher from the basement. Something – perhaps someone – was behind her. She almost felt a touch.

'Hallo, Mother!'

She knew her search was over.

'Alfred – oh, Alfred – where . . . how did . . . ?'

'But, Mother – I was driving the bus.'

THE DEAD SMILE

F. Marion Crawford

Sir Hugh Ockram smiled as he sat by the open window of his study, in the late August afternoon, and just then a curiously yellow cloud obscured the low sun, and the clear summer light turned lurid, as if it had been suddenly poisoned and polluted by the foul vapours of a plague. Sir Hugh's face seemed, at best, to be made of fine parchment drawn skintight over a wooden mask, in which two eyes were sunk out of sight, and peered from far within through crevices under the slanting, wrinkled lids, alive and watchful like two toads in their holes, side by side and exactly alike. But as the light changed, then a little yellow glare flashed in each. Nurse Macdonald said once that when Sir Hugh smiled he saw the faces of two women in hell – two dead women he had betrayed. (Nurse Macdonald was a hundred years old.) And the smile widened, stretching the pale lips across the discoloured teeth in an expression of profound self-satisfaction, blended with the most unforgiving hatred and contempt for the human doll. The hideous disease of which he was dying had touched his brain. His son stood beside him, tall, white, and delicate as an angel in a primitive picture, and though there was deep distress in his violet eyes as he looked at his father's face, he felt the shadow of that sickening smile stealing across his own lips and parting them and drawing them against his will. And it was like a bad dream, for he tried not to smile and smiled the more. Beside him, strangely like him in her wan, angelic beauty, with the same shadowy golden hair, the same sad violet eyes, the same luminously pale face, Evelyn Warburton rested one hand upon his arm. And as she looked into her uncle's eyes, and could not turn her own away, she knew that the deathly smile was hovering on her own red lips, drawing them tightly across her little teeth, while two bright tears ran down her cheeks to her mouth, and dropped from the upper to the lower lip while she smiled – and the smile was like the shadow of death and the seal of damnation upon her pure, young face.

'Of course,' said Sir Hugh very slowly, and still looking out at the trees, 'if you have made up your mind to be married, I cannot hinder you, and I don't suppose you attach the smallest importance to my consent –'

'Father!' exclaimed Gabriel reproachfully.

'No, I do not deceive myself,' continued the old man, smiling terribly. 'You will marry when I am dead, though there is a very good reason why you had better not – why you had better not,' he repeated very emphatically, and he slowly turned his toad eyes upon the lovers.

'What reason?' asked Evelyn in a frightened voice.

'Never mind the reason, my dear. You will marry just as if it did not exist.' There was a long pause. 'Two gone,' he said, his voice lowering strangely, 'and two more will be four – all together – for ever and ever, burning, burning, burning bright.'

At the last words his head sank slowly back, and the little glare of the toad eyes disappeared under the swollen lids, and the lurid cloud passed from the westering sun, so that the earth was green again and the light pure. Sir Hugh had fallen asleep, as he often did in his last illness, even while speaking.

Gabriel Ockram drew Evelyn away, and from the study they went out into the dim hall, softly closing the door behind them, and each audibly drew breath, as though some sudden danger had been passed. They laid their hands each in the other's, and their strangely-like eyes met in a long look, in which love and perfect understanding were darkened by the secret terror of an unknown thing. Their pale faces reflected each other's fear.

'It is his secret,' said Evelyn at last. 'He will never tell us what it is.'

'If he dies with it,' answered Gabriel, 'let it be on his own head!'

'On his head!' echoed the dim hall. It was a strange echo, and some were frightened by it, for they said that if it were a real echo it should repeat everything and not give back a phrase here and there, now speaking, now silent. But Nurse Macdonald said that the great hall would never echo a prayer when an Ockram was to die, though it would give back curses ten for one.

'On his head!' it repeated quite softly, and Evelyn started

and looked round.

'It is only the echo,' said Gabriel, leading her away.

They went out into the late afternoon light, and sat upon a stone seat behind the chapel, which was built across the end of the east wing. It was very still, not a breath stirred, and there was no sound near them. Only far off in the park a song-bird was whistling the high prelude to the evening chorus.

'It is very lonely here,' said Evelyn, taking Gabriel's hand nervously, and speaking as if she dreaded to disturb the silence. 'If it were dark, I should be afraid.'

'Of what? Of me?' Gabriel's sad eyes turned to her.

'Oh no! How could I be afraid of you? But of the old Ockrams – they say they are just under our feet here in the north vault outside the chapel, all in their shrouds, with no coffins, as they used to bury them.'

'As they always will – as they will bury my father, and me. They say an Ockram will not lie in a coffin.'

'But it cannot be true – these are fairy tales – ghost stories!' Evelyn nestled nearer to her companion, grasping his hand more tightly, and the sun began to go down.

'Of course. But there is a story of old Sir Vernon, who was beheaded for treason under James II. The family brought his body back from the scaffold in an iron coffin with heavy locks, and they put it in the north vault. But ever afterwards, whenever the vault was opened to bury another of the family, they found the coffin wide open, and the body standing upright against the wall, and the head rolled away in a corner, smiling at it.'

'As Uncle Hugh smiles?' Evelyn shivered.

'Yes, I suppose so,' answered Gabriel, thoughtfully. 'Of course I never saw it, and the vault has not been opened for thirty years – none of us have died since then.'

'And if – if Uncle Hugh dies – shall you – ' Evelyn stopped, and her beautiful thin face was quite white.

'Yes. I shall see him laid there too – with his secret, whatever it is.' Gabriel sighed and pressed the girl's little hand.

'I do not like to think of it,' she said unsteadily. 'Oh Gabriel, what can the secret be? He said we had better not marry – not that he forbade it – but he said it so strangely, and he smiled – ugh!' Her small white teeth chattered with fear, and she looked over her shoulder while drawing still closer to

Gabriel. 'And, somehow, I felt it in my own face – '

'So did I,' answered Gabriel in a low, nervous voice. 'Nurse Macdonald – ' He stopped abruptly.

'What? What did she say?'

'Oh – nothing. She has told me things – they would frighten you, dear. Come, it is growing chilly.' He rose, but Evelyn held his hand in both of hers, still sitting and looking up into his face.

'But we shall be married, just the same – Gabriel! Say that we shall!'

'Of course, darling – of course. But while my father is so very ill, it is impossible – '

'Oh Gabriel, Gabriel dear! I wish we were married now!' cried Evelyn in sudden distress. 'I know that something will prevent it and keep us apart.'

'Nothing shall!'

'Nothing?'

'Nothing human,' said Gabriel Ockram, as she drew him down to her.

And their faces, that were so strangely alike, met and touched – and Gabriel knew that the kiss had a marvellous savour of evil, but on Evelyn's lips it was like the cool breath of a sweet and mortal fear. And neither of them understood, for they were innocent and young. Yet she drew him to her by her lightest touch, as a sensitive plant shivers and waves its thin leaves, and bends and closes softly upon what it wants, and he let himself be drawn to her willingly, as he would if her touch had been deadly and poisonous; for she strangely loved that half voluptuous breath of fear, and he passionately desired the nameless evil something that lurked in her maiden lips.

'It is as if we loved in a strange dream,' she said.

'I fear the waking,' he murmured.

'We shall not wake, dear – when the dream is over it will have already turned into death, so softly that we shall not know it. But until then – '

She paused, and her eyes sought his, and their faces slowly came nearer. It was as if they had thoughts in their red lips that foresaw and foreknew the deep kiss of each other.

'Until then – ' she said again, very low, and her mouth was nearer to his.

'Dream – till then,' murmured his breath.

Nurse Macdonald was a hundred years old. She used to sleep sitting all bent together in a great old leathern arm-chair with wings, her feet in a bag footstool lined with sheepskin, and many warm blankets wrapped about her, even in summer. Beside her a little lamp always burned at night by an old silver cup, in which there was something to drink.

Her face was very wrinkled, but the wrinkles were so small and fine and near together that they made shadows instead of lines. Two thin locks of hair, that was turning from white to a smoky yellow again, were drawn over her temples from under her starched white cap. Every now and then she woke, and her eyelids were drawn up in tiny folds like little pink silk curtains, and her queer blue eyes looked straight before her through doors and walls and worlds to a far place beyond. Then she slept again, and her hands lay one upon the other on the edge of the blanket, the thumbs had grown longer than the fingers with age, and the joints shone in the low lamplight like polished crab-apples.

It was nearly one o'clock in the night, and the summer breeze was blowing the ivy branch against the panes of the window with a hushing caress. In the small room beyond, with the door ajar, the girl-maid who took care of Nurse Macdonald was fast asleep. All was very quiet. The old woman breathed regularly, and her indrawn lips trembled each time as the breath went out, and her eyes were shut.

But outside the closed window there was a face, and violet eyes were looking steadily at the ancient sleeper, for it was like the face of Evelyn Warburton, though there were eighty feet from the sill of the window to the foot of the tower. Yet the cheeks were thinner than Evelyn's, and as white as a gleam, and her eyes stared, and the lips were not red with life, they were dead and painted with new blood.

Slowly Nurse Macdonald's wrinkled eyelids folded themselves back, and she looked straight at the face at the window while one might count ten.

'Is it time?' she asked in her little old, far-away voice.

While she looked the face at the window changed, for the eyes opened wider and wider till the white glared all round the bright violet, and the bloody lips opened over gleaming teeth, and stretched and widened and stretched again, and the shadow golden hair rose and streamed against the window in the night breeze. And in answer to Nurse Macdonald's question came the sound that freezes the living flesh.

That low moaning voice that rises suddenly, like the scream of storm, from a moan to a wail, from a wail to a howl, from a howl to the fear-shriek of the tortured dead – he who had heard knows, and he can bear witness that the cry of the banshee is an evil cry to hear alone in the deep night. When it was over and the face was gone, Nurse Macdonald shook a little in her great chair, and still she looked at the black square of the window, but there was nothing more there, nothing but the night, and the whispering ivy branch. She turned her head to the door that was ajar, and there stood the girl in her white gown, her teeth chattering with fright.

'It is time, child,' said Nurse Macdonald. 'I must go to him, for it is the end.'

She rose slowly, leaning her withered hands upon the arms of the chair, and the girl brought her a woollen gown and a great mantle, and her crutch-stick, and made her ready. But very often the girl looked at the window and was unjointed with fear, and often Nurse Macdonald shook her head and said words which the maid could not understand.

'It was like the face of Miss Evelyn,' said the girl at last, trembling.

But the ancient woman looked up sharply and angrily, and her queer blue eyes glared. She held herself by the arm of the great chair with her left hand, and lifted up her crutch-stick to strike the maid with all her might. But she did not.

'You are a good girl,' she said, 'but you are a fool. Pray for wit, child, pray for wit – or else find service in another house than Ockram Hall. Bring the lamp and help me under my left arm.'

The crutch-stick clacked on the wooden floor, and the low heels of the woman's slippers clappered after her in slow triplets, as Nurse Macdonald got towards the door. And down the stairs each step she took was a labour in itself, and by the clacking noise the waking servants knew that she was coming, very long before they saw her.

No one was sleeping now, and there were lights and whisperings and pale faces in the corridors near Sir Hugh's bedroom, and now someone went in, and now someone came out, but every one made way for Nurse Macdonald, who had nursed Sir Hugh's father more than eighty years ago.

The light was soft and clear in the room. There stood Gabriel Ockram by his father's bedside, and there knelt Evelyn Warburton, her hair lying like a golden shadow down her shoulders, and her hands clasped nervously together. And opposite Gabriel, a nurse was trying to make Sir Hugh drink. But he would not, and though his lips were parted, his teeth were set. He was very, very thin and yellow now, and his eyes caught the light sideways and were as yellow coals.

'Do not torment him,' said Nurse Macdonald to the woman who held the cup. 'Let me speak to him, for his hour is come.'

'Let her speak to him,' said Gabriel in a dull voice.

So the ancient woman leaned to the pillow and laid the featherweight of her withered hand, that was like a brown moth, upon Sir Hugh's yellow fingers, and she spoke to him earnestly, while only Gabriel and Evelyn were left in the room to hear.

'Hugh Ockram,' she said, 'this is the end of your life; and as I saw you born, and saw your father born before you, I am come to see you die. Hugh Ockram, will you tell me the truth?'

The dying man recognized the little far-away voice he had known all his life, and he very slowly turned his yellow face to Nurse Macdonald; but he said nothing. Then she spoke again.

'Hugh Ockram, you will never see the daylight again. Will you tell the truth?'

His toad-like eyes were not dull yet. They fastened themselves on her face.

'What do you want of me?' he asked, and each word struck hollow on the last. 'I have no secrets. I have lived a good life.'

Nurse Macdonald laughed – a tiny, cracked laugh, that made her old head bob and tremble a little, as if her neck were on a steel spring. But Sir Hugh's eyes grew red, and his pale lips began to twist.

'Let me die in peace,' he said slowly.

But Nurse Macdonald shook her head, and her brown,

moth-like hand left his and fluttered to his forehead.

'By the mother that bore you and died of grief for the sins you did, tell me the truth!'

Sir Hugh's lips tightened on his discoloured teeth.

'Not on Earth,' he answered slowly.

'By the wife who bore your son and died heart-broken, tell me the truth!'

'Neither to you in life, nor to her in eternal death.'

His lips writhed, as if the words were coals between them, and a great drop of sweat rolled across the parchment of his forehead. Gabriel Ockram bit his hand as he watched his father die. But Nurse Macdonald spoke a third time.

'By the woman whom you betrayed, and who waits for you this night, Hugh Ockram, tell me the truth!'

'It is too late. Let me die in peace.'

The writhing lips began to smile across the set yellow teeth, and the toad eyes glowed like evil jewels in his head.

'There is time,' said the ancient woman. 'Tell me the name of Evelyn Warburton's father. Then I will let you die in peace.'

Evelyn started back, kneeling as she was, and stared at Nurse Macdonald, and then at her uncle.

'The name of Evelyn's father?' he repeated slowly, while the awful smile spread upon his dying face.

The light was growing strangely dim in the great room. As Evelyn looked, Nurse Macdonald's crooked shadow on the wall grew gigantic. Sir Hugh's breath came thick, rattling in his throat, as death crept in like a snake and choked it back. Evelyn prayed aloud, high and clear.

Then something rapped at the window, and she felt her hair rise upon her head in a cool breeze, as she looked around in spite of herself. And when she saw her own white face looking in at the window, and her own eyes staring at her through the glass, wide and fearful, and her own hair streaming against the pane, and her own lips dashed with blood, she rose slowly from the floor and stood rigid for one moment, till she screamed once and fell straight back into Gabriel's arms. But the shriek that answered hers was the fear-shriek of the tormented corpse, out of which the soul cannot pass for shame of deadly sins, though the devils fight in it with corruption, each for their due share.

Sir Hugh Ockram sat upright in his death-bed, and saw and cried aloud:

'Evelyn!' His harsh voice broke and rattled in his chest as he sank down. But still Nurse Macdonald tortured him, for there was a little life left in him still.

'You have seen the mother as she waits for you, Hugh Ockram. Who was this girl Evelyn's father? What was his name?'

For the last time the dreadful smile came upon the twisted lips, very slowly, very surely now, and the toad eyes glared red, and the parchment face glowed a little in the flickering light. For the last time words came.

'They know it in hell.'

Then the glowing eyes went out quickly, the yellow face turned waxen pale, and a great shiver ran through the thin body as Hugh Ockram died.

But in death he still smiled, for he knew his secret and kept it still, on the other side, and he would take it with him, to lie with him for ever in the north vault of the chapel where the Ockrams lie uncoffined in their shrouds – all but one. Though he was dead, he smiled, for he had kept his treasure of evil truth to the end, and there was none left to tell the name he had spoken, but there was all the evil he had not undone left to bear fruit.

As they watched – Nurse Macdonald and Gabriel, who held Evelyn still unconscious in his arms while he looked at the father – they felt the dead smile crawling along their own lips – the ancient crone and the youth with the angel's face. Then they shivered a little, and both looked at Evelyn as she lay with her head on his shoulder, and, though she was very beautiful, the same sickening smile was twisting her young mouth too, and it was like the foreshadowing of a great evil which they could not understand.

But by and by they carried Evelyn out, and she opened her eyes and the smile was gone. From far away in the great house the sound of weeping and crooning came up the stairs and echoed along the dismal corridors, for the women had begun to mourn the dead master, after the Irish fashion, and the hall had echoes of its own all that night, like the far-off wail of the banshee among forest trees.

When the time was come they took Sir Hugh in his winding-sheet on a trestle bier, and bore him to the chapel and through the iron door and down the long descent to the north vault, with tapers, to lay him by his father. And two men went in first to prepare the place, and came back staggering like drunken men, and white, leaving their lights behind them.

But Gabriel Ockram was not afraid, for he knew. And he went in alone and saw that the body of Sir Vernon Ockram was leaning upright against the stone wall, and that his head lay on the ground near by with the face turned up, and the dried leathern lips smiled horribly at the dried-up corpse, while the iron coffin, lined with black velvet, stood open on the floor.

Then Gabriel took the thing in his hands, for it was very light, being quite dried by the air of the vault, and those who peeped in from the door saw him lay it in the coffin again, and it rustled a little, like a bundle of reeds, and sounded hollow as it touched the sides and the bottom. He also placed the head upon the shoulders and shut down the lid, which fell to with a rusty spring that snapped.

After that they laid Sir Hugh beside his father, with the trestle bier on which they had brought him, and they went back to the chapel.

But when they saw one another's faces, master and men, they were all smiling with the dead smile of the corpse they had left in the vault, so that they could not bear to look at one another until it had faded away.

Gabriel Ockram became Sir Gabriel, inheriting the baronetcy with the half-ruined fortune left by his father, and still Evelyn Warburton lived at Ockram Hall, in the south room that had been hers ever since she could remember anything. She could not go away, for there were no relatives to whom she could have gone, and, besides, there seemed to be no reason why she should not stay. The world would never trouble itself to care what the Ockrams did on their Irish estates, and it was long since the Ockrams had asked anything of the world.

So Sir Gabriel took his father's place at the dark old table in the dining-room, and Evelyn sat opposite to him, until such time as their mourning should be over, and they might be married at last. And meanwhile their lives went on as before, since Sir Hugh had been a hopeless invalid during the last year of his life, and they had seen him but once a day for the little while, spending most of their time together in a strangely perfect companionship.

But though the late summer saddened into autumn, and autumn darkened into winter, and storm followed storm, and rain poured on rain through the short days and the long nights, yet Ockram Hall seemed less gloomy since Sir Hugh had been laid in the north vault beside his father. And at Christmastide Evelyn decked the great hall with holly and green boughs, and huge fires blazed on every hearth. Then the tenants were all bidden to a New Year's dinner, and they ate and drank well, while Sir Gabriel sat at the head of the table. Evelyn came in when the port wine was brought, and the most respected of the tenants made a speech to propose her health.

It was long, he said, since there had been a Lady Ockram. Sir Gabriel shaded his eyes with his hand and looked down at the table, but a faint colour came into Evelyn's transparent cheeks. But, said the grey-haired farmer, it was longer still since there had been a Lady Ockram so fair as the next was to be, and he gave the health of Evelyn Warburton.

Then the tenants all stood up and shouted for her, and Sir Gabriel stood up likewise, beside Evelyn. And when the men gave the last and loudest cheer of all there was a voice not theirs, above them all, higher, fiercer, louder – a scream not earthly, shrieking for the bride of Ockram Hall. And the holly and the green boughs over the great chimney-piece shook and slowly waved as if a cool breeze were blowing over them. But the men turned very pale, and many of them set down their glasses, but others let them fall upon the floor for fear. And looking into one another's faces, they were all smiling strangely, a dead smile, like dead Sir Hugh's. One cried out words in Irish, and the fear of death was suddenly upon them all so that they fled in panic, falling over one another like wild beasts in the burning forest, when the thick smoke runs along before the flame, and the tables were overset, and drinking glasses and bottles were broken in heaps, and the dark red wine crawled like blood upon the polished floor.

Sir Gabriel and Evelyn stood alone at the head of the table before the wreck of the feast, not daring to turn to see each other, for each knew that the other smiled. But his right arm held her and his left hand clasped her right as they stared before them, and but for the shadows of her hair one might not have told their two faces apart. They listened long, but the cry came not again, and the dead smile faded from their lips, while each remembered that Sir Hugh Ockram lay in the north vault, smiling in his winding-sheet, in the dark, because he had died with his secret.

So ended the tenants' New Year's dinner. But from that time on Sir Gabriel grew more and more silent, and his face grew even paler and thinner than before. Often without warning and without words, he would rise from his seat, as if something moved him against his will, and he would go out into the rain or the sunshine to the north side of the chapel, and sit on the stone bench, staring at the ground as if he could see through it, and through the vault below, and through the white winding-sheet in the dark, to the dead smile that would not die.

Always when he went out in that way Evelyn came out presently and sat beside him. Once, too, as in summer, their beautiful faces came suddenly near, and their lids drooped, and their red lips were almost joined together. But as their eyes met, they grew wide and wild, so that the white showed in a ring all round the deep violet, and their teeth chattered, and their hands were like hands of corpses, each in the other's for the terror of what was under their feet, and of what they knew but could not see.

Once, also, Evelyn found Sir Gabriel in the chapel alone, standing before the iron door that led down to the place of death, and in his hand there was the key to the door, but he had not put it in the lock. Evelyn drew him away, shivering, for she had also been driven in waking dreams to see that terrible thing again, and to find out whether it had changed since it had lain there.

'I'm going mad,' said Sir Gabriel, covering his eyes with his hand as he went with her. 'I see it in my sleep, I see it when I am awake – it draws me to it, day and night – and unless I see it I shall die!'

'I know,' answered Evelyn, 'I know. It is as if threads were spun from it, like a spider's, drawing us down to it.' She was silent for a moment, and then she started violently and grasped his arm with a man's strength, and almost screamed the words she spoke. 'But we must not go there!' she cried. 'We must not go!'

Sir Gabriel's eyes were half shut, and he was not moved by the agony of her face.

'I shall die, unless I see it again,' he said, in a quiet voice not like his own. And all that day and that evening he scarcely spoke, thinking of it, always thinking, while Evelyn Warburton quivered from head to foot with a terror she had never known.

She went alone, on a grey winter's morning, to Nurse Macdonald's room in the tower, and sat down beside the great leathern easy-chair, laying her thin white hand upon the withered fingers.

'Nurse,' she said, 'what was it that Uncle Hugh should have told you, that night before he died? It must have been an awful secret – and yet, though you asked him, I feel somehow that you know it, and that you know why he used to smile so dreadfully.'

The old woman's head moved slowly from side to side.

'I only guess – I shall never know,' she answered slowly in her cracked little voice.

'But what do you guess? Who am I? Why did you ask who my father was? You know I am Colonel Warburton's daughter, and my mother was Lady Ockram's sister, so that Gabriel and I are cousins. My father was killed in Afghanistan. What secret can there be?'

'I do not know. I can only guess.'

'Guess what?' asked Evelyn imploringly, and pressing the soft withered hands, as she leaned forward. But Nurse Macdonald's wrinkled lids dropped suddenly over her queer blue eyes, and her lips shook a little with her breath, as if she were asleep.

Evelyn waited. By the fire the Irish maid was knitting fast, and the needles clicked like three or four clocks ticking against each other. And the real clock on the wall solemnly ticked alone, checking off the seconds of the woman who was a hundred years old, and had not many days left. Outside the ivy branch beat the window in the wintry blast, as it had beaten against the glass a hundred years ago.

Then as Evelyn sat there she felt again the waking of a

horrible desire – the sickening wish to go down, down to the thing in the north vault, and to open the winding-sheet, and see whether it had changed, and she held Nurse Macdonald's hands as if to keep herself in her place and fight against the appalling attraction of the evil dead.

But the old cat that kept Nurse Macdonald's feet warm, lying always on the bag footstool, got up and stretched itself, and looked up into Evelyn's eyes, while its back arched, and its tail thickened and bristled, and its ugly pink lips drew back in a devilish grin, showing its sharp teeth. Evelyn stared at it, half fascinated by its ugliness. Then the creature suddenly put out one paw with all its claws spread, and spat at the girl, and all at once the grinning cat was like the smiling corpse far down below, so that Evelyn shivered down to her small feet, and covered her face with her free hand lest Nurse Macdonald should wake and see the dead smile there, for she could feel it.

The old woman had already opened her eyes again, and she touched her cat with the end of her crutch-stick, whereupon its back went down and its tail shrunk, and it sidled back to its place on the bag footstool. But its yellow eyes looked up sideways at Evelyn, between the slits of its lids.

'What is it that you guess, nurse?' asked the young girl again.

'A bad thing – a wicked thing. But I dare not tell you, lest it might not be true, and the very thought should blast your life. For if I guess right, he meant that you should not know, and that you two should marry, and pay for his old sin with your souls.'

'He used to tell us that we ought not to marry – '

'Yes – he told you that, perhaps – but it was as if a man put poisoned meat before a starving beast and said, "Do not eat", but never raised his hand to take the meat away. And if he told you that you should not marry, it was because he hoped you would, for of all men living or dead, Hugh Ockram was the falsest man that ever told a cowardly lie, and the cruellest that ever hurt a weak woman, and the worst that ever loved a sin.'

'But Gabriel and I love each other,' said Evelyn, very sadly.

Nurse Macdonald's old eyes looked far away, at sights seen long ago, and that rose in the grey winter air amid the mists of an ancient youth.

'If you love, you can die together,' she said, very slowly. 'Why should you live, if it is true? I am a hundred years old. What has life given me? The beginning is fire, the end is a heap of ashes, and between the end and the beginning lies all the pain in the world. Let me sleep, since I cannot die.'

Then the old woman's eyes closed again, and her head sank a little lower upon her breast.

So Evelyn went away and left her asleep, with the cat asleep on the bag footstool; and the young girl tried to forget Nurse Macdonald's words, but she could not, for she heard them over and over again in the wind, and behind her on the stairs. And as she grew sick with fear of the frightful unknown evil to which her soul was bound, she felt a bodily something pressing her, and pushing her, and forcing her on, and from the other side she felt the threads that drew her mysteriously, and when she shut her eyes, she saw in the chapel behind the altar, the low iron door through which she must pass to go to the thing.

And as she lay awake at night, she drew the sheet over her face, lest she should see shadows on the wall beckoning her and the sound of her own warm breath made whisperings in her ears, while she held the mattress with her hands, to keep from getting up and going to the chapel. It would have been easier if there had not been a way thither through the library, by a door which was never locked. It would be fearfully easy to take her candle and go softly through the sleeping house. And the key of the vault lay under the altar behind a stone that turned. She knew the little secret. She could go alone and see.

But when she thought of it, she felt her hair rise on her head, and first she shivered so that the bed shook, and then the horror went through her in a cold thrill that was agony again, like myriads of icy needles, boring into her nerves.

The old clock in Nurse Macdonald's tower struck midnight.

From her room she could hear the creaking chains and weights in their box in the corner of the staircase, and overhead the jarring of the rusty lever that lifted the hammer. She had heard it all her life. It struck eleven strokes clearly and then came the twelfth, with a dull half stroke, as though the hammer were too weary to go on, and had fallen asleep against the bell.

The old cat got up from the bag footstool and stretched itself, and Nurse Macdonald opened her ancient eyes and looked slowly round the room by the dim light of the night lamp. She touched the cat with her crutch-stick, and it lay down upon her feet. She drank a few drops from her cup and went to sleep again.

But downstairs Sir Gabriel sat straight up as the clock struck, for he had dreamed a fearful dream of horror, and his heart stood still, till he awoke at its stopping, and it beat again furiously with his breath, like a wild thing set free. No Ockram had ever known fear waking, but sometimes it came to Sir Gabriel in his sleep.

He pressed his hands to his temples as he sat up in bed, and his hands were icy cold, but his head was hot. The dream faded far, and in its place there came the master thought that racked his life; with the thought also came the sick twisting of his lips in the dark that would have been a smile. Far off, Evelyn Warburton dreamed that the dead smile was on her mouth, and awoke, starting with a little moan, her face in her hands shivering.

But Sir Gabriel struck a light and got up and began to walk up and down his great room. It was midnight, and he had barely slept an hour, and in the north of Ireland the winter nights are long.

'I shall go mad,' he said to himself, holding his forehead. He knew that it was true. For weeks and months the possession of the thing had grown upon him like a disease, till he could think of nothing without thinking first of that. And now all at once it outgrew his strength, and he knew that he must be its instrument or lose his mind – that he must do the deed he hated and feared, if he could fear anything, or that something would snap in his brain and divide him from life while he was yet alive. He took the candlestick in his hand, the old-fashioned heavy candlestick that had always been used by the head of the house. He did not think of dressing, but went as he was, in his silk night-clothes and his slippers, and he opened the door. Everything was very still in the great old house. He shut the door behind him and walked noiselessly on the carpet through the long corridor. A cool breeze blew over his shoulder and blew the flame of his candle straight out from him. Instinctively he stopped and looked round, but all was still, and the upright flame burned steadily. He walked on, and instantly a strong draught was behind him, almost extinguishing the light. It seemed to blow him on his way, ceasing whenever he turned, coming again when he went on – invisible, icy.

Down the great staircase to the echoing hall he went, seeing nothing but the flaring flame of the candle standing away from him over the guttering wax, while the cold wind blew over his shoulder and through his hair. On he passed through the open door into the library, dark with old books and carved bookcases, on through the door in the shelves, with painted shelves on it, and the imitated backs of books, so that one needed to know where to find it – and it shut itself after him with a soft click. He entered the low-arched passage, and though the door was shut behind him and fitted tightly in its frame, still the cold breeze blew the flame forward as he walked. And he was not afraid, but his face was very pale, and his eyes were wide and bright, looking before him, seeing already in the dark air the picture of the thing beyond. But in the chapel he stood still, his hand on the little turning stone tablet in the back of the stone altar. On the tablet were engraved words, '*Clavis sepulchri Clarissimorum Dominorum De Ockram*' – ('the key to the vault of the most illustrious lords of Ockram'). Sir Gabriel paused and listened. He fancied that he heard a sound far off in the great house where all had been so still, but it did not come again. Yet he waited at the last, and looked at the low iron door. Beyond it, down the long descent, lay his father uncoffined, six months dead, corrupt, terrible in his clinging shroud. The strangely preserving air of the vault could not yet have done its work completely. But on the thing's ghastly features, with their half-dried, open eyes, there would still be the frightful smile with which the man had died – the smile that haunted –

As the thought crossed Sir Gabriel's mind, he felt his lips writhing, and he struck his own mouth in wrath with the back of his hand so fiercely that a drop of blood ran down his chin and another, and more, falling back in the gloom upon the chapel pavement. But still his bruised lips twisted themselves. He turned the tablet by the simple secret. It needed no safer fastening, for had each Ockram been confined in pure gold, and had the door been wide, there was not a man in Tyrone brave enough to go down to that place, saving Gabriel Ockram himself, with his angel's face and his thin, white hands, and his sad unflinching eyes. He took the great gold key and set it into the lock of the iron door, and the heavy, rattling noise echoed down the descent beyond like footsteps, as if a watcher had stood behind the iron and were running away within, with heavy dead feet. And though he was standing still, the cool wind was from behind him, and blew the flame of the candle against the iron panel. He turned the key.

Sir Gabriel saw that his candle was short. There were new ones on the altar, with long candlesticks, and he lit one, and left his own burning on the floor. As he set it down on the pavement his lip began to bleed again, and another drop fell upon the stones.

He drew the iron door open and pushed it back against the chapel wall, so that it should not shut of itself, while he was within, and the horrible draught of the sepulchre came up out of the depths in his face, foul and dark. He went in, but though the fetid air met him, yet the flame of the tall candle was blown straight from him against the wind while he walked down the easy incline with steady steps, his loose slippers slapping the pavement as he trod.

He shaded the candle with his hand, and his fingers seemed to be made of wax and blood as the light shone through them. And in spite of him the unearthly draught forced the flame forward, till it was blue over the black wick, and it seemed as if it must go out. But he went straight on, with shining eyes.

The downward passage was wide, and he could not always see the walls by the struggling light, but he knew when he was in the place of death by the larger, drearier echo of his steps in the greater space and by the sensation of a distant blank wall. He stood still, almost enclosing the flame of the candle in the hollow of his hand. He could see a little, for his eyes were growing used to the gloom. Shadowy forms were outlined in the dimness, where the biers of the Ockrams stood crowded together, side by side, each with its straight, shrouded corpse, strangely preserved by the dry air, like the empty shell that the locust sheds in summer. And a few steps before him he saw clearly the dark shape of headless Sir Vernon's iron coffin, and he knew that nearest to it lay the thing he sought.

He was as brave as any of those dead men had been, and they were his fathers, and he knew that sooner or later he should lie there himself, beside Sir Hugh, slowly drying to a parchment shell. But he was still alive, and he closed his eyes a moment, and three great drops stood on his forehead.

Then he looked again, and by the whiteness of the winding-sheet he knew his father's corpse, for all the others were brown with age; and, moreover, the flame of the candle was blown towards it. He made four steps till he reached it, and suddenly the light burned straight and high, shedding a dazzling yellow glare upon the fine linen that was all white, save over the face, and where the joined hands were laid on the breast. And at those places ugly stains had spread, darkened with outlines of the features and of the tight-clasped fingers. There was a frightful stench of drying death.

As Sir Gabriel looked down, something stirred behind him, softly at first, then more noisily, and something fell to the stone floor with a dull thud and rolled up to his feet; he started back, and saw a withered head lying almost face upward on the pavement, grinning at him. He felt the cold sweat standing on his face, and his heart beat painfully.

For the first time in all his life that evil thing which men call fear was getting hold of him, checking his heart-strings as a cruel driver checks a quivering horse, clawing at his backbone with icy hands, lifting his hair with freezing breath, climbing up and gathering in his midriff with leaden weight.

Yet presently he bit his lip and bent down, holding the candle in one hand, to lift the shroud back from the head of the corpse with the other. Slowly he lifted it. Then it clove to the half-dried skin of the face, and his hand shook as if someone had struck him on the elbow, but half in fear and half in anger at himself, he pulled it, so that it came away with a little ripping sound. He caught his breath as he held it, not yet throwing it back, and not yet looking. The horror was working in him, and he felt that old Vernon Ockram was standing up in his iron coffin, headless, yet watching him with the stump of his severed neck.

While he held his breath he felt the dead smile twisting his lips. In sudden wrath at his own misery, he tossed the death-stained linen backward, and looked at last. He ground his teeth lest he should shriek aloud.

There it was, the thing that haunted him, that haunted Evelyn Warburton, that was like a blight on all that came near him.

The dead face was blotched with dark stains, and the thin, grey hair was matted about the discoloured forehead. The sunken lids were half open, and the candlelight gleamed on something foul where the toad eyes had lived.

But yet the dead thing smiled, as it had smiled in life; the ghastly lips were parted and drawn wide and tight upon the wolfish teeth, cursing still, and still defying hell to do its worst – defying, cursing, and always and for ever smiling alone in the dark.

Sir Gabriel opened the winding-sheet where the hands were, and the blackened, withered fingers were closed upon something stained and mottled. Shivering from head to foot, but fighting like a man in agony for his life, he tried to take the package from the dead man's hold. But as he pulled at it the claw-like fingers seemed to close more tightly, and when he pulled harder the shrunken hands and arms rose from the corpse with a horrible look of life following his motion – then as he wrenched the sealed packet loose at last, the hands fell back into their place still folded.

He set down the candle on the edge of the bier to break the seals from the stout paper. And, kneeling on one knee, to get a better light, he read what was within, written long ago in Sir Hugh's queer hand.

He was no longer afraid.

He read how Sir Hugh had written it all down that it might perchance be a witness of evil and of his hatred; how he had loved Evelyn Warburton, his wife's sister; and how his wife had died of a broken heart with his curse upon her, and how Warburton and he had fought side by side in Afghanistan, and Warburton had fallen; but Ockram had brought his comrade's wife back a full year later, and little Evelyn, her child, had been born in Ockram Hall. And next, how he had wearied of the mother, and she had died like her sister with his curse on her. And then, how Evelyn had been brought up as his niece, and how he had trusted that his son Gabriel and his daughter, innocent and unknowing, might love and marry, and the souls of the women he had betrayed might suffer another anguish before eternity was out. And, last of all, he hoped that some day, when nothing could be undone, the two might find his writing and live on, not daring to tell the truth for their children's sake and the world's word, man and wife.

This he read, kneeling beside the corpse in the north vault, by the light of the altar candle; and when he had read it all, he thanked God aloud that he had found the secret in time. But when he rose to his feet and looked down at the dead face it was changed, and the smile was gone from it for ever, and the jaw had fallen a little, and the tired, dead lips were relaxed. And then there was a breath behind him and close to him, not cold like that which had blown the flame of the candle as he came, but warm and human. He turned suddenly.

There she stood, all in white, with her shadowy golden hair – for she had risen from her bed and had followed him noiselessly, and had found him reading, and had herself read over his shoulder. He started violently when he saw her, for his nerves were unstrung – and then he cried out her name in the still place of death:

'Evelyn!'

'My brother!' she answered, softly and tenderly, putting out both hands to meet his.

CRIMSON LAKE

Daphne Froome

Rex and Owen Ainsworth sat facing Mr T. Payne of Dutton Pugh and Payne, Solicitors and Commissioners for Oaths, in a rather breathless but total silence; a silence that contrasted sadly, Mr Payne thought, with the strident demise of Mark Banks, whose affairs the two young men had come to discuss.

It was Rex who spoke at last. 'We're sorry of course about Mr Banks, but this really is the most marvellous piece of luck for us.'

'You're fortunate he never bothered to update his will,' answered Mr Payne, 'so the portion of the estate which was meant for his friend, your late uncle Mr D. Ainsworth – that is the Banks Playhouse plus ten thousand pounds – now automatically passes to both of you jointly as Mr Ainsworth's nearest relatives.'

'It's a pity we never met Mr Banks – what was he like?' asked Owen.

'I was not very well acquainted with him. I'm afraid he was a very unsociable person.'

'But surely you were the one who found him just after he died?' Rex remarked.

Mr Payne endeavoured to reply calmly. 'Yes,' he said, 'but that was really by chance – you see, he would never answer any correspondence I sent to his flat so I took to calling in at the theatre whenever any urgent legal matter needed attention. It was on one such occasion . . .' Mr Payne paused.

'Perhaps you could tell us something about the Banks Playhouse,' said Rex.

'Oh, he was much concerned with that theatre of his,' replied Mr Payne, 'though it was the electrical side that interested him most: he was quite fanatical about it. On one occasion he even beat up a stage-hand for meddling with a couple of switches. But that need not bother you; I'd advise you to sell up and forget all about it.'

'But we intend to use the theatre for our band,' said Rex.

'It's called Crimson Lake,' put in Owen proudly.

Mr Payne suppressed a shudder. 'Good heavens! Well, I hope you realize all the difficulties involved. Have you a manager?'

'Oh, Rex is our manager,' Owen replied. 'He's always had to look after me so he's capable of shouldering the most crippling of responsibilities. He's an electronics engineer so he also looks after our electronics. We have mikes, lights, all the usual gear. I'm sure he's quite up to Mr Banks's standard.'

'How do we get there? When can we move in?' Rex queried impatiently. He was slightly older and more businesslike than his brother.

'I have the keys here so you can go along now if you like,' Mr Payne replied.

'Great,' said Owen. 'We ought to get going because we left our van outside, parked on a yellow line.'

Mr Payne watched with some trepidation as they hurried away. Their visit had brought back vividly to him the memory of the dead, stiff figure of Mark Banks as he lay alone in the deserted theatre. Indeed the hideous vision the man had presented, dressed in shabby jeans and plimsolls, with his long hair curling down over the collar of an old sweater dotted with solder, and the shattering sound of the taped music that had played on and on to his deaf ears were all too easily recalled to Mr Payne. He sometimes wondered if he would ever be rid of them.

Rex and Owen regarded the boarded-up frontage of the theatre with some disappointment.

'Well, it's certainly well barricaded,' Owen remarked. 'What instructions did Mr Payne give?'

'We go in by the back, down Bright Lane,' Rex said.

Even before Rex had finished parking the van, Owen was unlocking the padlock on one of the theatre doors and sending it creaking and rattling open. 'Can you bring the torch out of the dashboard? It's very gloomy in here and I can't find the switch.' His voice came muffled from inside the building.

Rex took the torch over and, shining it round, soon found a switch; then, depressing it, gently illuminated the auditorium with the dusty light from two very elegant glass chandeliers suspended from the ceiling.

Owen let out an exclamation. 'It's like a Victorian Music

Hall! Gold plush seats and a red carpet – no one warned us it would be like this. It wouldn't be so bad if it weren't for the gaudy orange tassels on the exit curtains.'

'Ah, but look at the ceiling,' Rex said, 'that's modern and new. I'm willing to bet he had that replaced in order to improve the acoustics. It's all certainly worth plenty of money and I've an idea our customers will love it – and it's not too large: just the right size, I'd say, for us at the moment.'

'We can always modernize it later on,' Owen added. 'Now I'd like to see what lies behind the safety curtain. The stage will probably be hung with silken backcloths and decorated with pillars of specially imported Italian marble.'

They found the stage just as it had been left after the last performance, with the stage manager's table still set up in the wings on one side and the prompter's chair on the other. Four screens bearing strange, psychedelic patterns stood in front of two gauze backcloths, hung one behind the other and painted in strongly-hued luminous paint.

'It's very violent,' said Owen. 'Over the edge, even for Crimson Lake, I should say.'

Rex was already making his way downstairs to the green-room. In it he found none of the usual props, but instead the place, together with its adjoining dressing-room, was crammed with equipment stacked carefully around the walls and arranged in neatly-labelled envelopes in the drawers of metal filing cabinets.

The ancient parquet flooring, reduced to rough wooden cobblestones by years of maltreatment beneath a variety of heavy props, rattled rather uncomfortably beneath his feet as he systematically went round the room exploring all the apparatus. The sudden discovery of so much valuable electronic equipment came as yet another pleasant shock to Rex – but the rickety floor would have to be repaired: merely walking across it had set the needle on one of the dials swinging. He returned to look at it more closely. It had swung right over. He wished the lighting were better – the one small electric bulb was less than adequate and he couldn't really check the dial because there were shadows everywhere, reflecting in the glass face, resolving themselves into strange, eerie shapes: into the shape of a person, a man with untidy long grey hair that surrounded a face that was hardly a face at all.

just eye sockets and one grim line where the mouth should have been . . .

He flung open the door and called for Owen, but there was no reply. Owen was probably in the gallery by now, finding out more about the theatre, as *he* should be doing instead of imagining shapes in shadows; it was only a reaction after all the excitement lately. He went determinedly back into the room – it really was not so dark after all, especially now the light from the corridor was streaming in, and the recalcitrant needle was once again nestling comfortably over the zero. He locked the door and went back into the auditorium.

Later on, when they were driving back down Bright Lane, Rex suddenly exclaimed, 'Blast, I've left the torch in the theatre. We might need it.'

Jumping from the van, Owen disappeared at a run. It was not long before he returned to find Rex waiting at the junction to the main road.

'I negotiated the alley much easier this time,' Rex remarked.

'Better than you did the lights in the theatre,' Owen replied. 'It's just as well I went back. You're a fine one, Rex. You left them all on. We'll never balance our books that way.'

'I didn't leave them on. I remember quite distinctly switching them off. The building was in darkness when I went away. If you didn't trust me you shouldn't have gone and left me to lock up.'

'I was only looking round the outside.'

'Well, I'm quite positive I switched them off.'

'And I'm quite positive you nearly collided with that taxi. Really, all the excitement *has* gone to your head.'

Rex, frowning, turned his attention to the rush-hour traffic.

'I'm glad you've warmed the place up for us,' remarked Hank, the drummer. He was a short, square man, inclined to be dour. 'After being empty for so long, I was expecting it to strike cold and damp.'

'Well, *I'm* not responsible,' answered Rex irritably. 'Owen must have switched it on by mistake yesterday when he came back for the torch.' The affair of the lights still rankled.

'Don't be petty,' Owen replied rather heatedly. Rex went to help him sort everything out. It took him and the four members of the band some time but at last they had the instruments and electronics all ready for their first rehearsal in these unusual surroundings.

After the band had started playing, Rex began to wander around, noting the effect in different parts of the auditorium. He wished he could listen to tunes as other folks did, but his training in the reproduction of music led him always to hear, over and above the rendering of any melody, the discordant subtleties of the electronic sound.

He concentrated for a moment on the two guitars, played by Brian and Owen, wondering if a little less treble on Brian's guitar would improve the contrast between them; but he knew he must be careful not to offend Brian who liked the sound as it was. He was very prone to stage fright, and the last thing Rex wanted to do was to upset him now. Rex was not quite happy, either, with the exact volume of the drum, which varied considerably depending where he sat, but then Hank's ebullient personality could be relied upon to distract the audience from any minor shortcomings – he always transformed his role as percussionist into a kind of individual virtuoso performance. Mike, ever meticulous, had already pointed out that one of the keyboard units was causing a touch of distortion. He would have to deal with that.

Seating himself in the centre of the stalls he leaned back and closed his eyes, listening carefully.

Suddenly there was a scream, a crash and a thud, and Rex's deliberations ended abruptly as, opening his eyes wide, he witnessed the spectacle of Hank's solid shape writhing and swearing upon the floor.

By the time Rex had reached the stage the others had already gathered round the drummer, who could be heard muttering over and over again in a kind of bemused mumble, 'It was an electric shock I tell you – I got a hell of a shock – off that drum case – '

'He can't really have done, can he?' Owen asked Rex. 'Those drums aren't connected up to anything. He must have imagined it.' He turned again to Hank. 'Pull yourself together, man; this is not like you – you're behaving like Brian.'

'Thank you very much,' Brian retorted and went over to stand sulking in a corner of the stage.

Rex helped Mike to raise Hank to a sitting position. 'Have

you noticed his hand?' asked Mike, addressing Rex across the still-shaking form of the drummer. 'Look at it – it's burnt. It couldn't possibly have been like that before. He could never have played with a hand like this.'

'Of course I couldn't, any fool can see that. It was a shock, I tell you,' Hank maintained. 'I'm not going near that drum again until you've checked it, Rex.'

Owen came over to Rex and asked anxiously, 'Well, what do you make of it?'

'I can't understand what happened,' Rex replied shortly.

No one was in the mood to continue the rehearsal, so the band agreed to finish for the day and go back to the hotel, leaving Rex behind to lock up.

After they had gone, Rex went over and examined the drum carefully. He could find nothing wrong with it at all. He had thought perhaps it might have picked up a stray current from somewhere, a wire trailing from one of the other instruments, perhaps, but there were no wires anywhere near it.

It was unbearably hot, he thought; he must go and switch off the heating or *he* would be collapsing.

Just at that moment he caught a glimpse of a distant figure in the wings opposite. This was all he needed, Rex decided, an interloper prowling about the place. As Rex moved towards it the figure, climbing a ladder with spectacular agility, disappeared on to a platform set about fifteen feet above the stage. By the time Rex reached the platform the figure had leapt to one of the lighting beams. But as Rex surveyed the drop, wondering if he dared follow, the figure faded – became insubstantial – a mere mass of cobwebs before his eyes –

He decided that he really *was* overwrought; but he must try to conceal the state of his nerves from Owen. Angrily he made his way back down the ladder and threw the heating switch to 'off' with malicious force.

Fortunately Hank was soon well enough to play again, though for more than a week after the incident he refused to go near his drums until Rex had checked them.

But with so much work to do in preparation for the opening night there was little time for worrying, and the spirits of the band rose steadily.

Rex had large numbers of posters printed, and now photographs of the band smiled down from hoardings, rode by on buses and gazed out from shop windows, greeting them every time they ventured out.

Rex bought a smart new suit and interviewed people in his office.

It had been his idea to take over one of the boxes adjacent the stage for his electronics. A box was out of the way, he maintained, yet a convenient place from which to run the leads to the stage and at the same time keep an eye on the performance. Rex also engaged an assistant named Bob to help him.

They had a final rehearsal on the morning of the performance. Owen took them through the music very smoothly. With Mike only a shade more meticulous in his manner, Brian hardly more edgy, and Hank barely more flamboyant than usual, Rex began to look forward to the evening quite confidently.

Then suddenly the control console exploded.

It was a very spectacular explosion, certainly one that not even Rex, with his concern for the first-night nerves of the band, could easily minimize. 'It's not a very serious fault,' he called down rather unconvincingly. 'It looked and sounded worse than it is.'

'Well, if you say so,' answered Owen doubtfully. 'We're nearly through; we could take this opportunity to have a break.'

He made his way round to Rex's box and gazed rather apprehensively at the smoking ruins of the console. 'Are you sure you can get it working in time?'

'Oh yes. I must say it worried me at first, but it's only the console, and they're quite easy to replace. There happens to be one that will serve our purpose among the electronics Mr Banks left behind. I'll need you and Bob to help me.'

Rex led the way downstairs to the green-room. The room full of apparatus fascinated him so much that he had spent many hours there and knew by now every component and where it was stored.

'It's just as well Mr Banks isn't around,' said Owen. 'He certainly wouldn't approve of you swiping one of his consoles.'

Rex went over to a large desk-like object with dials and

slider controls. 'This is what we need. Bob, Owen, you'll have to give me a hand.'

As soon as they had carried the control console up into the box, Rex and Bob began carefully connecting it up while Owen took the band to lunch. Except for the small clinks of the components and the occasional remarks of the two men as they worked, the theatre was very quiet until, in just over an hour, with the work completed, the electronics hummed into life.

Rex and Bob sat in their box observing with considerable pleasure, tempered by now with more than a little apprehension, the gathering audience. There was a rustle as the curtain rose and the spectators took in the spacious elegance of the set. Owen, who always designed the sets, had decided on a backdrop of panelled wooden screens. He had placed Mike, with his splendid collection of keyboard instruments, on the left of the stage and Hank and the percussion on a slightly raised platform to the right. A staircase, curving up to this platform, continued upwards again to a semicircular walk around which Owen and Brian could progress as they played. This, together with the constantly varying lighting, gave a feeling of movement to the performance which seemed now to Rex to flow as smoothly and flawlessly as he or any of the band could have wished.

The distinguished audience settled down into an appreciative silence – the first half ended in very enthusiastic applause.

Rex left Bob in charge and hurried round to Owen's dressing-room. 'Congratulations,' he said.

'You're rather premature in your rejoicing,' Owen answered shortly. 'Brian, the fool, has left the Indian bells and the tambourine at the hotel. We shan't be able to do the last number without them.'

'Well, for heaven's sake don't be cross with him,' answered Rex. 'You know how nervous he gets. Tell him I'll go and fetch them at once. Say he can rely on me to have them back here in plenty of time.'

'What about the electronics? Do you think you should leave them after what happened this morning?'

'It's all working perfectly and Bob is quite capable of taking charge for a few minutes. If I go now I'll be back almost before the end of the first number.'

Rex, driving the van out into the main road, found the traffic almost at a standstill. It look him longer, too, than he had anticipated to collect the instruments from Owen's room, and almost three-quarters of an hour had elapsed before he arrived back at the theatre. He was rather agitated but still in plenty of time.

Tonight the court behind the theatre was brightly lit, but there was no one about. He would have expected Owen to have detailed someone to await his arrival – he supposed in all the hustle he had forgotten.

Rex carried the instruments in through the stage door and the sound of the music met him as he made his way along. The band was certainly creating a record number of decibels tonight, he decided, and what a beat! They did not seem to be varying the tune much, though; not at all, in fact, for they were playing the same few notes over and over again. Perhaps Brian had been overcome by one of his bouts of stage fright and upset the whole band. Suddenly apprehensive, Rex began to run towards the stage. The sight that met his astounded gaze as he arrived froze him, all movement arrested.

The members of the band had obviously been working desperately for some time; sweat stood out on their faces, their crimson silk shirts, purchased specially for the occasion, were wrinkled and soiled, but the figures inside them were hardly moving now, they merely lurched slowly, lethargically, almost grotesquely, from side to side, in time with the inexorable beat. Owen and Brian were standing together at the back of the stage, supporting themselves by hanging drunkenly on to the microphone stands, whilst Mike and Hank slumped back in their chairs.

But it was really the sight of the instruments that riveted Rex's attention. The strings and keys vibrated out the sound, the drum pulsed continuously on and on, but all without any human aid. Sparks flashed across from one of the abandoned guitars to the other, round and round the drums in circles, and in peculiar patterns of light and shade over the keyboards. And the beat went on and on . . .

And out in the auditorium the audience, completely mesmerized, a sea of stupified, dead white faces, watched without the slightest trace of movement.

The hypnotic hammering of the rhythm began to take a hold on Rex's senses too, setting the scene dancing and vibrating before his eyes. He staggered on to the stage just in time to catch Owen as he lurched forward towards the sparking electronics. In a half-stunned daze he managed to drag Brian and Owen to the back of the stage where he left them, propped up against the smart new wooden screens, gazing at him through clouded eyes.

Then, with his hands clasped over his ears, he made his way round to his box where he found Bob, stone-like and senseless, surrounded by a smell of hot electronic casing and overburdened wires.

Rex reached over towards the panel of slider switches on the new console he had only that afternoon put into use. His one idea was to decrease the volume, but there seemed to be a strange force acting on the switches, pushing them up as fast as he tried to pull them down. It was striving to keep the volume just high enough to drive everyone rapidly towards insanity, yet staying just within the capacity of the electronics. In such equilibrium Rex was perfectly aware that it could go on for hours without bringing about its own destruction.

He renewed his hold on the sliding switches and began to force them slowly downwards. As he did so a faint shadow appeared, and gradually taking shape, grew slowly stronger until it resolved itself into the figure of an elderly man, wearing his hair untidily long. It stood in the front of the box, and so close did it come to Rex as it leant over the console facing him, that he could even make out the blobs of what looked like solder standing out on a worn blue jersey; and the hands that were battling to force up the switches were large and serviceable, carrying with them a terrible strength. There did not seem to be any eyes in the face, only deep, unfathomable sockets that bored through Rex's consciousness; the mouth was pursed in a hard, determined line that etched deep creases into what was already yellow wrinkled skin.

With one last effort, Rex forced the switches further and further down, holding them still. The volume of sound became less but the expression on the diabolical face was unmoved, merely concentrating on building up a force that Rex could not possibly hope to match.

He held on. The beat was reasonably quiet now, but as

steady and determined as ever. The forces were mounting. Rex pressed the slides down even further . . .

Suddenly he released his hold.

The volume surged up and the spectral face before him split into a horrible grimace of surprise, then, with a flash and sheet of flame, the whole of the electronics disintegrated and Rex experienced an agony of pain that sent him catapulting right through the misty figure, over the edge of the box and down into the stalls below.

He landed amidst the insensible audience, sending them over like wooden skittles. Some of them, jerked into a kind of motor-like movement by the impact of his body, and others, woken by the sudden silence, began to file out. Row by row the rest followed, in front of the advancing flames.

Rex, lying across the seats, was almost casually picked up and carried out by two eminent music critics who afterwards, somewhat biased by their part in his rescue, gave the band an almost hysterically effusive write-up which did more to ensure its future success than any other single event.

Mr Payne visited the band in hospital looking paternal and carrying a bouquet of expensive flowers in one hand and a large collection of newspapers in the other.

He commiserated with them all on the state of the theatre, enquiring anxiously about the progress of Owen, Mike, Hank and Brian who assured him that they were all recovering rapidly from the shock and minor burns they had suffered; and he spent a considerable time convincing himself that neither Rex's broken leg nor his state of concussion was at all serious.

Rex's slightly wan smile, even though it emanated from a face black with bruises, seemed to reassure Mr Payne, who now pointed out the banner headlines in the newspapers.

'You're all very famous,' he said. 'The press has taken a happy line between the excellence of your performance and the really extraordinary circumstances that preceded the fire. No one seems at all clear what happened, you know.'

Rex said carefully, 'The audience was thoroughly enthralled by the music. You must admit that, Mr Payne, you were there.'

'To tell you the truth, I don't remember . . .' Mr Payne

suddenly looked very worried and became silent.

'Well,' said Owen, 'it's a good thing there were no serious casualties, and, as for the theatre, it was well insured. Anyway, I've a feeling we shall need something rather larger than the Banks Playhouse for our performances in the future. We'd like you to help us sell it as soon as possible.'

Mr Payne suddenly looked very relieved. 'I am pleased about that,' he said, 'very pleased.'

'That's settled then,' said Rex. 'I must say we shan't be sorry to see the back of it ourselves.'

The new owner of the Banks Playhouse stood surveying his acquisition with pride. The insurance company had paid up very well and he was pleased with the economical way the repairs had been carried out after the fire – why, they had hardly entailed any outlay at all. He had even been able to use the original wiring. The electricians had assured him it was excellent, not, he was convinced, like the amateurish circuits created by those young pop stars who had been the cause of the fire.

The building was in more capable hands now. It was gay too, the way he had it arranged. 'BINGO', it stated in bright red fairy lights over the entrance, and inside more lights winked joyfully in blue, yellow, mauve and green. Completely trouble free, it was, almost as if it worked by itself!

OLD SHADOWS

Ken Alden

I have always known that there was something strange about my old family home, but it was only recently that I fully realized what it was. My childhood was a happy one. From the hill of middle-age I look down upon an Eden where life is one long day of games and entertainment, but alas, cursed by the relentless snake of time, which will eventually drive me out.

Memories are tinged with a rosy glow: afternoon teas with aged great-aunts in old-fashioned costumes, warm peaceful summer days when I played with my two sisters on a daisy-covered lawn that was surrounded by dahlias and lilac trees. The ghosts of my toys came gliding up the avenue of time – the Teddy-bear with one ear, the train set, the plywood fort and the red fire engine that rang its bell when wound up. Then there is Tobias the cat that once scratched my arm, two caged birds that never sang, and of course – Nana. She was a large collie dog with long black and white hair. We called her Nana because she bore some resemblance to the dog in *Peter Pan*; always looking after us, always ready to join in our rough-and-tumble games – this is a very clear memory – and becoming extremely agitated whenever I attempted to climb a tree.

It was not until we started visiting the homes of our friends that my sisters and I realized that there was something wrong with Grange Park. They did not have parents who were in a state of constant anxiety, servants who gave notice after a few weeks, to say nothing of a cook who steadfastly refused to come up from her basement kitchen.

I think we were perceptive enough to understand that it was not arguments or anything of that kind that disturbed our parents' peace of mind. It was something about the house itself; a 'something' that was perceptible to adults only and not to us.

But there was one occasion, when we were playing with Nana in the nursery, which started a line of unrewarding conjecture in – at least – my mind. Suddenly the girl who was acting as our nanny came into the room, widened her eyes until they became blue lakes of abject terror, then screamed before running from the room. We never saw her again. One of my sisters was of the opinion this strange outburst was the result of a bilious attack – an ailment that often laid Cook low – but I decided that there must be more to it than an unwise diet, and in consequence questioned my mother.

'Mother, why was Nanny so frightened?'

For a while it seemed that she had not heard my all-important question, then she drew me to her and began to speak in that patronizing tone that adults often use when talking to children.

'Your uncle used to own this house and he had a little boy who was about your age.'

This was most interesting and I demanded more information.

'Where is this little boy?'

My mother sighed deeply and it was some time before she provided an answer.

'He would climb one of the oak trees in the garden. He fell – and was killed.'

I thought this was meant to be a warning for me not to climb trees, lest I too came to such a calamitous end, and hastened to reassure my mother.

'I will never climb a tree. Nana won't let me.'

My mother closed her eyes, then opened them again.

'Well, dear – Nana was your cousin's dog. Do you understand?'

I nodded. 'Yes. That's why Nana won't let me climb a tree.'

Mother tightened her grip on my arm. 'But – your cousin died over twenty years ago.'

I gave this statement my full consideration and came to a not unreasonable conclusion.

'Then Nana must be very old. Very old for a dog.'

Mother released me, then stood up. 'Yes, dear – very old. Now go out and play.'

And that's the nearest I ever came to being told the truth.

The years passed. I went to boarding school and when I came home at the end of the first term, Nana had mysteriously disappeared, although when I mentioned this fact to my youngest sister, she said:

'Don't be silly. I saw her this morning.'

I did not pursue the subject – indeed there was a strange reluctance to do so – and when the holiday came to an end, Nana had receded back into the mists of dying childhood. Truthfully, I do not think I thought of her again until last year, when I paid a much overdue visit to my mother.

After my father's death she left the old house and moved into a small bungalow which was part of a building estate nearby. She lived there all alone, my sisters having followed me to London and foreign parts long before Father died. One perished in a fire, the other now lived in South Africa.

As I expected, the visit turned out to be a particularly embarrassing one. We sat facing one another, sipping lukewarm tea and nibbling crumbling biscuits, and a wall of silence seemed to be looming up between us. I could not think of anything interesting to say. It is perhaps to my shame that I had been away from my family so long, Mother had become merely an elderly stranger. She started to talk about relatives – most of them long since dead – but the names meant little to me. There were a number of faces that smiled – or frowned – at me through the mist of time, but none of them could be united with a name. Suddenly I realized that there was a topic of conversation that would be of mutual interest. The house. I raised my voice because Mother had grown a little deaf.

'I passed the old house on my way here. It's in a bad state and there's a To-be-Sold sign by the front gate.'

My mother shook her head sadly. 'I knew those Matthew people would never stay. I did not like them, but they were the only ones who could afford a decent price.'

'Remember when Anne fell in the pond?' I asked. 'Nana got herself in a right old state and went running round the edge like a hen frightened for her chicks.'

Mother frowned. 'Nana! Who was Nana?'

'Why,' I exclaimed in genuine surprise, 'the dog. The black and white collie. You must remember.'

She placed her tea cup and saucer gently down on an occasional table, then said gently:

'You must be mistaken, dear. Your dear father would never allow a dog in the house.'

In retrospect I cannot believe she was deliberately trying

to evade the issue, but had long since thrust an unpleasant piece of information back into the dark caverns of the subconscious. Now, in old age, she was quite unable to bring it back into the light of memory.

After a while she said:

'I'm sure you were all very happy in the house. I know I was – for most of the time.'

Then the wall of silence sprang up between us again and after several futile attempts to open other lines of conversation, I left.

The estate agent knew my family well so there was little trouble in obtaining the front door key, and thus prolonging my visit to the past. The house seemed much smaller than I remembered and bore only a superficial resemblance to the home of my childhood. Peeling paintwork, crumbling mortar, broken windows – the ruthless ogre of time, assisted by its left-hand sister neglect, had not dealt kindly with Grange Park. Even the garden seemed to have shrunk to half its original size. The oak tree I had once tried to climb was gone, and the pond was a mere patch of mud. The once smooth lawn was now a mass of tangled grass and golden-faced dandelions that bowed their heads as though begging largesse from the sun.

Once in the house I tried to refurnish the damp, empty rooms with the frail fabric of memory, but it was a hopeless task. I looked sadly at the festoons of cobwebs that partially hid the cracked ceilings and the dust-covered floorboards, and knew the house was in its death throes. Soon the demolishers would move in and where the dying giant had once stood, would be rows of neat, red-roofed pygmies.

I walked along the hall and descended the stairs that led to the kitchen, while half expecting to hear Cook's raucous voice announcing her irrevocable intention of never leaving her subterranean domain. Here little rocks of identification rose up from the grey sea of dead memories that washes the shores of yesteryear and the ever-shifting land of now. The empty fireplace where the great iron range had once stood; the long slate shelves on which Cook had once kept her copper saucepans; the big larder – which was now coated with some unpleasant fungi.

I stood in the middle of the vast underground space – it no longer warranted the title of room – and tried to call up the ghosts of the distant past, but to no avail. Cook – who surely would have made a solid phantom – did not materialize and go floating across the floor to her empty larder. Neither did Anne come wailing from the past, demanding butter and sympathy, as on the occasion when she had burnt her fingers on the not-to-be-touched hotplate. I turned about and slowly climbed the stairs.

Back in the hall I tasted the silence that was broken only by the mournful sighing of the never-resting wind. That at least had not changed. I was about to leave when another sound came from somewhere above and beyond the great staircase. A soft bump, followed by a slow creak of an opening door.

Fear came out of the empty rooms and fastened cold claws on my shoulders. I wanted to run from that house and take refuge in warm crowded places, but at the same time there was a strange, almost morbid curiosity that demanded I mount those stairs and find out what – or who – had made the sounds. At the back of my mind was the thought that there must be a mundane explanation and if I could discover it, then all would be well and fear could retreat into the brooding shadows and free me to walk bravely under the noonday sun.

Stairboards creaked and startled small life that scuttled across the dust-carpeted floor. The landing drew gradually nearer and it seemed as if I heard the childish laughter, the high-pitched young voices – the occasional scream of mock alarm. When I had mounted the last stair, came up on to the landing and stood facing the nursery door, I distinctly heard a boy's voice – oh, merciful God! my own – cry out:

'Really, Anne, you are the giddy limit!'

I ran forward and pushed open that door, took one further, faltering step into the room and peered into the gloomy interior. It was empty. My sigh went shuddering back along the misty avenue of time and was lost in the awful void of eternity. Presently I turned and took a firm grip of the mouldering doorpost – then became as fearful as a sinful man on Judgement Day.

Nana was standing a mere two feet away.

She was as real as Monday morning. Long black and white

hair, bright, love-filled eyes, head raised, tail swaying gently back and forth. When she moved towards me, I screamed. One long-drawn-out scream that went echoing through the old house and had not died away when I stumbled down the stairs and set up a sprint record for the front door.

Now, after a lapse of twelve months, I can feel only pity for that canine shade that walks the desolate corridors, mourning the long-departed children it can no longer protect, and it is difficult to imagine why Nana should have inspired so much fear. After all, her intentions were of the best.

Troubled by this thought I wrote to Anne and gave her a full account of my experience. The following is an extract taken verbatim from her reply.

'. . . I heard Cook talking to one of our many nannies when I was about six and only recently has the gist of that conversation made sense. It wasn't Nana who frightened them. Why should she? She was a gentle ghost. No – it was the vision of a middle-aged man who stood in the nursery doorway and silently screamed.'

THE MAN WITH THE FLUTE

Rosemary Timperley

I am at school again now and everything seems ordinary. But I am not listening to this boring lesson. I am thinking about what happened during the past few weeks. As I sit at my desk, wearing my 'attentive' expression, which I fix on like a mask for the benefit of the teacher, I am talking silently to you in my head – telling you all about it, as if I were speaking aloud – because it was exciting and wonderful, and no one can ever, ever convince me that it wasn't.

He *did* exist, my Man with the Flute!

It started three weeks ago. Christmas was over but I was still on holiday. Dad and Mother had both gone back to work. They don't get such long holidays as schoolchildren and teachers do. So I was left on my own during the daytimes. My parents didn't really like this situation, but there was no alternative. Anyway, I'm twelve years old – it's not as if I were a little girl. I'm fine on my own. In fact, I liked having the flat to myself when they were out. It made me feel grown-up. As if it were *my* flat.

I even 'made myself useful'. I'd wash the breakfast-things for a start, then make the beds: the chores Mother usually managed to do when I was at school – but why should she when I was still on holiday? I liked helping, so she let me.

But these bits of so-called housework don't last long. By ten or ten-thirty in the morning, I'd be finished – washing-up done, beds made, a bit of dusting performed, just the surfaces of things – why look for dust in corners? Leave it in peace, that's what I say. Dust has as much right to live as anyone else.

And then I'd have the whole day before me, until five p.m. when Mother came back from the factory, where she made paper flowers. (The benefit of this was that we always had free paper flowers in the house – all the colours of the rainbow, and all sorts of flowers – roses, carnations, violets, snowdrops, gladioli, the lot. We were decorated all the year round.)

Well, the chores done, I'd read for a bit, then listen to the radio and dance to the dance music, and sing with the pop singers, and learn the words of the songs . . . and then I'd go for a walk before lunch. Mother made me promise always to have lunch, even if I wasn't hungry, and to take a walk to get up an appetite. She left a set lunch for me – bread, cheese, and a glass of lemon juice – 'Protein, fat, carbohydrate and Vit. C,' she said.

She was a very conscientious mother, although she went out to work. I know other people say otherwise, but it's not so.

It was on my dutiful walk, to 'get up an appetite', that I first saw the Man with the Flute.

He was standing in the street, not far from the block where we live. He was old, white hair blowing in the wind, shabby clothes, himself very thin and scraggy – and his hands looked almost like skeleton-hands as they pressed the stops on his flute. But the music he produced was not old. It was young as youth. It was full of zest and excitement. I'd go for my walk feeling quite old, but after hearing a few notes of his flute, I'd feel like a little tiny kid dancing among the daisies . . .

Not that I'd ever done such a thing, but that shows how young it was. Magical-young.

That first time I saw and heard him, I just looked at him and passed by. I was too shy to speak. Same the second and third times. But on the fourth day, I didn't pass. I plucked up my courage and stood in front of him. It was a very cold day. A fleck of snow in the air – too cold for a real snowfall. Everyone else was hurrying and scurrying, wrapped up in scarves and hoods, and some even had umbrellas up to protect them from the bits of snow. Only the Man with the Flute and I were standing still. He was still, playing. I was still, silent.

Then he stopped playing and looked into my eyes.

No one has ever looked so deeply into my eyes before. I expect that is mostly because I never look into other people's eyes myself. I'm afraid that they will see more of what I'm like than I shall see what they're like. And I never want anyone to see into *me*. No one must look through *my* windows.

But he did. He looked so hard into my windows that I had to look back into his. We started staring each other out.

I don't know which of us won for suddenly the snow broke. A real deluge of it. It broke the still coldness, and it broke our staring. He raised his flute to his lips again and went on playing, as if I wasn't there. I ran home.

I said nothing about him to my parents. I don't really know why – except that he was mysteriously important to me, and – again I don't know why – one never says anything *important* to one's parents, does one? They must always be kept out of it, whatever it is.

On the following day, I went to look for him.

My duty-walk before lunch was a pleasure now – a quest.

There he was, standing on the kerb, almost ankle deep in snow, playing his flute. The music soared, like bird-song. He himself looked rather like a featherless and starved bird, shoulders hunched high, spindly legs black-outlined against the snowy road behind him.

Again I stopped in front of him. At the same moment, snow began to fall again, big, sloppy white flakes of it – rather warming in a funny way. Slippety-sloppety.

I said, 'Are you hungry?'

He stopped playing and nodded his head.

'Then come home with me and share my lunch.'

I started back home and beckoned him to follow. I half-expected him not to – but he did. There was only one weird thing about him. As we plodded along, me first, him following, I left a trail of footprints in the snow, but he did not. I thought maybe that was the effect flute-playing had on people. How was I to know that it was *really* weird? After all, everything is weird! Life itself for a start! You can't keep picking on every little thing . . .

I led him up the stairs and into our flat. I wiped my feet on the mat, as I'd been most severely taught to do. He didn't bother. But nor did he leave any mess. I told him to sit down at the kitchen table, and I divided my lunch in half, half for him, half for me. Then I sat down opposite him and he was looking into my eyes again. And again I had to look back.

Then he spoke.

'You've forgotten me,' he said.

'Forgotten you? Oh, no! I've thought of you for hours, ever since yesterday.'

'I mean – you've forgotten that other time.'

'What other time?'

'We were young,' he said.

'I still am.'

'Not "still". Again.'

'Eat your lunch.' My voice, in my own ears, sounded a little like my mother's, when she was telling me to eat. How funny . . .

But he didn't eat. 'I'm not hungry for that,' he said. 'It was you I wanted, you I came back to talk to, but you don't remember. The experiment has failed. I must go back.' He got up and walked out. Soundlessly. I ran after him to the front door. I did not see it open or close, but he had gone. And then, faintly, I heard his flute playing in the street outside. I went to the window and looked out. But the snowfall was blinding. I saw nothing but fragmented whiteness.

When my mother came home at five, tired and snow-soaked, I told her nothing. I put on my act of being just as usual, an ordinary schoolgirl on holiday – who had 'been a good girl' and 'eaten up her lunch, every bit' – and next day I went out to look for him, my Man with the Flute.

The snow had stopped falling but lay like a white carpet underfoot. A pale-primrose sun struggled to peer through clouds. The Man with the Flute was not in his usual place, but I could hear his music in the distance. I walked in the direction of the sound, but each time I drew closer to it, it moved farther away. I seemed to be under a kind of spell as I followed the music. I thought of Browning's poem, 'The Pied Piper', which we'd done at school. The children who followed him had vanished for ever. Perhaps I would vanish too. Where did one go if one vanished? A reasoning part of me began to struggle against the lure of the music, but it wasn't strong enough. I knew that I was drawing farther and farther away from home, that the streets around me had ceased to be familiar, that I had no idea where I was or how I'd get back – but still I followed, followed. There's a song, 'Come, follow, follow . . .'. I must have been following for hours, as afternoon darkness was beginning to fall. The sun had vanished behind the tall houses like a dropped light. But the music still played in the dark and still I followed. Time had collapsed for me. This, I felt, could go on for ever.

Then there was a change. Instead of continuing to retreat, the flute-sound ahead of me stayed still. I was actually overtaking it at last – and when I reached the source of the sound, the Man with the Flute would be there.

I reached the source of the sound. It was loud and clear

and very close. The flute seemed to be right against my ear. The Man must be there in the dark, but I couldn't see him – not so much as a glimmer of his white hair, a gleam of his strange, deep eyes. There was nothing but solitude and the closeness of the music.

And then the music stopped.

And the spell broke.

I was aware that it was bitterly cold, that I was exhausted, that my feet were soaked and frozen from the long snow-walk, and that I was lost. Worse than that, it was night. I should be at home. My parents would be worried sick! I must have been mad to carry on like this! I really felt quite ill. I had to find someone. So, desperation beating back natural shyness, I went up to the front door of the house opposite where the music had stopped. I rang the bell. A light was switched on in the hall. The door opened. 'Who is it?' a woman's voice asked cautiously.

'Please,' I said, trying to sound less frantic than I felt, 'I've been so silly – I've got myself lost in the dark streets – I don't know where I am – and I'm freezing cold . . .'

The door opened wide. 'Oh, you poor child. Come right in.'

A nice woman, about my mother's age. She called her husband. 'Tom, it's a little girl lost!' She took me into the living-room where the man rose to greet me – and I got the shock of my life, for he was very like a younger, plumper edition of the Man with the Flute. And suddenly the mystery seemed solved to me. The Man with the Flute was perhaps this man's father, and lived here, and that was why the music had stopped and he had vanished. He had simply come indoors. Certain that this was what had happened, I said impulsively: 'I followed the Man with the Flute. He lives here with you, doesn't he?'

There was a shocked silence, as if I'd uttered some dreadful swear-word. The couple were looking at me in wonder. Then, 'You'd better sit down,' the woman said. 'I'll fetch you a hot drink. You're not quite yourself. Tom, help her to take off those wet shoes and dry them before the fire.'

She bustled out of the room.

'What have I said to make you both look like that?' I asked. 'Doesn't he live here? Or is it a secret? If it is, you needn't worry about me. I haven't told anyone about him.'

'Why did you come here?' he asked, helping me off with my shoes, and his deep eyes seemed so familiar.

'I told you. I followed the music. Is it your father? You're so like him.'

'My father did live here with us. He died this time last year.'

'Then my Man couldn't be him, could he?' But I had gone very cold, and I was remembering the way my Man had made no footprints and had left our flat without opening and closing the front door and how his eyes had gazed from some other world than this.

'Did he – play the flute – your father?' I whispered.

'Yes. He was a professional flautist. Then he grew old and couldn't get work, so he used to go out and play in the street. Not for money. Just to be listened to by many people. My wife and I couldn't stop him. It was what he wanted to do, and he had a strong will. But he went out in all weathers and it was too much for him. He caught a cold which was more than a cold, died of pneumonia. And you – you say you followed – someone – here?'

I nodded. 'I used not to believe in ghosts,' I said, 'but I think that's what he must have been. His music had a very funny effect on me. Well, look at what's happened – here I am – miles away from home – all through following the music. Did you hear it?'

The man nodded. 'Yes. Very faintly. I did hear it. But my wife did not.'

'You're his son – you *would* hear – there'd be a connection between you and him – but what could there be between him and me? Why me?'

'I'm going to show you a photograph of my father as a child, with his sister.' He brought an album from the bookcase and opened it at an old-fashioned picture of two children, hand in hand. One was a boy of about fourteen, the other a girl of about twelve – and she looked so like me that I gasped with astonishment.

And then I recalled that queer conversation at the flat, when my Man had said: 'You've forgotten me . . . You've forgotten that other time . . . We were young.' And later, 'It was you I wanted, you I came back to talk to, but you don't remember. The experiment has failed. I must go back.' And I had not seen him since, only heard his music – the music which had led me to this house.

'She is like me, isn't she?' I said. 'I suppose she's an old lady now.'

'No. She died of tuberculosis when she was still a child, not long after that photograph was taken. TB is curable nowadays. It wasn't then. Many children died of it. But my father had adored his little sister and he never got over her loss. Even in the last years of his life, he composed special tunes on his flute for her. He believed that she still existed in some other sphere, as a soul, waiting for a home. He believed in reincarnation – that is, to put it very simply, that a soul after the death of the body returns to the world in another body . . .'

His wife came in with a cup of hot chocolate. 'Tom, what nonsense are you telling the child?' she said. 'Have you no tact?' She removed the album. 'Just because this little girl looks rather like – like someone else – ' She handed me the hot drink. 'Get that inside you, child, then Tom will drive you home.'

'She's had a very strange experience,' said Tom, then changed the subject. His wife had made him feel foolish. I felt rather foolish too. Everything became ordinary again.

After I'd had my drink, Tom got his car out of the garage and drove me to the flat. He came up with me to explain what had happened, although we agreed between us that we wouldn't mention the Man with the Flute. We would simply say that I had gone for a long walk, got lost, and called at his house for help. It was true, in its fashion.

My parents were so relieved to see me that I didn't get too much of a scolding. I was sent straight to bed. I heard the others talking in the living-room; brooded mistily over the events of the day, then slept.

'The most extraordinary thing,' my mother said next morning. 'That nice man who brought you home – it turns out that we're distantly related. His great-grandfather was the brother of my great-grandmother, and it seems that you have a marked physical resemblance to one of his aunts who died young. The two sides of the family lost touch with each other generations ago, but now we've met up again – and all because you went for a long walk and got lost. Isn't it an amazing coincidence?'

'Yes, isn't it,' I agreed, knowing at the same time that it had not been a coincidence at all – that I had been taken to that house, led there, by a magic spell cast by the music of the Man with the Flute.

On the following Sunday we went to tea with our new-found relations. My parents exclaimed at the similarity of the child in the old photograph to myself. They put it down to heredity, of course. Tom said not a word about reincarnation. Nor did I. And neither of us mentioned the Man with the Flute. Tom's wife merely said that her father-in-law had once played in orchestras, but that was all. It's as if grown-ups are afraid of strange things. Even Tom seemed to regret having spoken to me so freely at that curiously intimate moment when he was drying my shoes before the fire.

And now, as I said, I am back at school, thinking about it all. It is a mystery which I may never solve, but I'm glad it happened. It was so interesting, and has opened my mind to all sorts of possibilities about life: other lives, other worlds – everything!

THE TAIPAN

W. Somerset Maugham

No one knew better than he that he was an important person. He was number one in not the least important branch of the most important English firm in China. He had worked his way up through solid ability and he looked back with a faint smile at the callow clerk who had come out to China thirty years before. When he remembered the modest home he had come from, a little red house in a long row of little red houses, in Barnes, a suburb which, aiming desperately at the genteel, achieves only a sordid melancholy, and compared it with the magnificent stone mansion, with its wide verandas and spacious rooms, which was at once the office of the company and his own residence, he chuckled with satisfaction. He had come a long way since then. He thought of the high tea to which he sat down when he came home from school (he was at St Paul's), with his father and mother and his two sisters, a slice of cold meat, a great deal of bread and butter and plenty of milk in his tea, everybody helping himself, and then he thought of the state in which now he ate his evening meal. He always dressed and whether he was alone or not he expected the three boys to wait at table. His number one boy knew exactly what he liked and he never had to bother himself with the details of housekeeping; but he always had a set dinner with soup and fish, entrée, roast, sweet, and savoury, so that if he wanted to ask anyone in at the last moment he could. He liked his food and he did not see why when he was alone he should have less good a dinner than when he had a guest.

He had indeed gone far. That was why he did not care to go home now, he had not been to England for ten years, and he took his leave in Japan or Vancouver, where he was sure of meeting old friends from the China coast. He knew no one at home. His sisters had married in their own station, their husbands were clerks and their sons were clerks; there was nothing between him and them; they bored him. He satisfied the claims of relationship by sending them every Christmas a piece of fine silk, some elaborate embroidery, or a case of tea. He was not a mean man and as long as his mother lived he had made her an allowance. But when the time came for him to retire he had no intention of going back to England, he had seen too many men do that and he knew how often it was a failure; he meant to take a house near the racecourse in Shanghai: what with bridge and his ponies and golf he expected to get through the rest of his life very comfortably. But he had a good many years before he need think of retiring. In another five or six Higgins would be going home and then he would take charge of the head office in Shanghai. Meanwhile he was very happy where he was, he could save money, which you couldn't do in Shanghai, and have a good time into the bargain. This place had another advantage over Shanghai: he was the most prominent man in the community and what he said went. Even the consul took care to keep on the right side of him. Once a consul and he had been at loggerheads and it was not he who had gone to the wall. The taipan thrust out his jaw pugnaciously as he thought of the incident.

But he smiled, for he felt in an excellent humour. He was walking back to his office from a capital luncheon at the Hong-Kong and Shanghai Bank. They did you very well there. The food was first-rate and there was plenty of liquor. He had started with a couple of cocktails, then he had some excellent sauterne, and he had finished up with two glasses of port and some fine old brandy. He felt good. And when he left he did a thing that was rare with him; he walked. His bearers with his chair kept a few paces behind him in case he felt inclined to slip into it, but he enjoyed stretching his legs. He did not get enough exercise these days. Now that he was too heavy to ride it was difficult to get exercise. But if he was too heavy to ride he could still keep ponies, and as he strolled along in the balmy air he thought of the spring meeting. He had a couple of griffins that he had hopes of and one of the lads in his office had turned out a fine jockey (he must see they didn't sneak him away, old Higgins in Shanghai would give a pot of money to get him over there) and he ought to pull off two or three races. He flattered himself that he had the finest stable in the city. He pouted his broad chest like a pigeon. It was a beautiful day, and it was good to be alive.

He paused as he came to the cemetery. It stood there, neat and orderly, as an evident sign of the community's opulence. He never passed the cemetery without a little glow of pride. He was pleased to be an Englishman. For the cemetery stood in a place, valueless when it was chosen, which with the increase of the city's affluence was now worth a great deal of money. It had been suggested that the graves should be moved to another spot and the land sold for building, but the feeling of the community was against it. It gave the taipan a sense of satisfaction to think that their dead rested on the most valuable site on the island. It showed that there were things they cared for more than money. Money be blowed! When it came to 'the things that mattered' (this was a favourite phrase with the taipan), well, one remembered that money wasn't everything.

And now he thought he would take a stroll through. He looked at the graves. They were neatly kept and the pathways were free from weeds. There was a look of prosperity. And as he sauntered along he read the names on the tombstones. Here were three side by side: the captain, the first mate, and the second mate of the barque *Mary Baxter*, who had all perished together in the typhoon of 1908. He remembered it well. There was a little group of two missionaries, their wives and children, who had been massacred during the Boxer troubles. Shocking thing that had been! Not that he took much stock in missionaries; but, hang it all, one couldn't have these damned Chinese massacring them. Then he came to a cross with a name on it he knew. Good chap, Edward Mulock, but he couldn't stand his liquor, drank himself to death, poor devil, at twenty-five; the taipan had known a lot of them do that; there were several more neat crosses with a man's name on them and the age, twenty-five, twenty-six, or twenty-seven; it was always the same story: they had come out to China; they had never seen so much money before, they were good fellows and they wanted to drink with the rest: they couldn't stand it, and there they were in the cemetery. You had to have a strong head and a fine constitution to drink drink for drink on the China coast. Of course it was very sad, but the taipan could hardly help a smile when he thought how many of those young fellows he had drunk underground. And there was a death that had been useful, a fellow in his own firm, senior to him and a clever chap too: if that fellow had lived he might not have been taipan now. Truly the ways of fate were inscrutable. Ah, and here was little Mrs Turner, Violet Turner, she had been a pretty little thing, he had had quite an affair with her; he had been devilish cut up when she died. He looked at her age on the tombstone. She'd be no chicken if she were alive now. And as he thought of all those dead people a sense of satisfaction spread through him. He had beaten them all. They were dead and he was alive, and by George he'd scored them off. His eyes collected in one picture all those crowded graves and he smiled scornfully. He very nearly rubbed his hands.

'No one ever thought I was a fool,' he muttered.

He had a feeling of good-natured contempt for the gibbering dead. Then, as he strolled along, he came suddenly upon two coolies digging a grave. He was astonished, for he had not heard that anyone in the community was dead.

'Who the devil's that for?' he said aloud.

The coolies did not even look at him, they went on with their work, standing in the grave, deep down, and they shovelled up heavy clods of earth. Though he had been so long in China he knew no Chinese, in his day it was not thought necessary to learn the damned language, and he asked the coolies in English whose grave they were digging. They did not understand. They answered him in Chinese and he cursed them for ignorant fools. He knew that Mrs Broome's child was ailing and it might have died, but he would certainly have heard of it, and besides, that wasn't a child's grave, it was a man's and a big man's too. It was uncanny. He wished he hadn't gone into that cemetery; he hurried out and stepped into his chair. His good-humour had all gone and there was an uneasy frown on his face. The moment he got back to his office he called to his number two:

'I say, Peters, who's dead, d'you know?'

But Peters knew nothing. The taipan was puzzled. He called one of the native clerks and sent him to the cemetery to ask the coolies. He began to sign his letters. The clerk came back and said the coolies had gone and there was no one to ask. The taipan began to feel vaguely annoyed: he did not like things to happen of which he knew nothing. His own boy would know, his boy always knew everything, and he sent for him; but the boy had heard of no death in the community.

'I knew no one was dead,' said the taipan irritably. 'But what's the grave for?'

He told the boy to go to the overseer of the cemetery and find out what the devil he had dug a grave for when no one was dead.

'Let me have a whisky and soda before you go,' he added, as the boy was leaving the room.

He did not know why the sight of the grave had made him uncomfortable. But he tried to put it out of his mind. He felt better when he had drunk the whisky, and he finished his work. He went upstairs and turned over the pages of *Punch*. In a few minutes he would go to the club and play a rubber or two of bridge before dinner. But it would ease his mind to hear what his boy had to say and he waited for his return. In a little while the boy came back and he brought the overseer with him.

'What are you having a grave dug for?' he asked the overseer point-blank. 'Nobody's dead.'

'I no dig glave,' said the man.

'What the devil do you mean by that? There were two coolies digging a grave this afternoon.'

The two Chinese looked at one another. Then the boy said they had been to the cemetery together. There was no new grave there.

The taipan only just stopped himself from speaking.

'But damn it all, I saw it myself,' were the words on the tip of his tongue.

But he did not say them. He grew very red as he choked them down. The two Chinese looked at him with their steady eyes. For a moment his breath failed him.

'All right. Get out,' he gasped.

But as soon as they were gone he shouted for the boy again, and when he came, maddeningly impassive, he told him to bring some whisky. He rubbed his sweating face with a handkerchief. His hand trembled when he lifted the glass to his lips. They could say what they liked, but he had seen the grave. Why, he could hear still the dull thud as the coolies threw the spadefuls of earth on the ground above them. What did it mean? He could feel his heart beating. He felt strangely ill at ease. But he pulled himself together. It was all nonsense.

If there was no grave there it must have been a hallucination. The best thing he could do was to go to the club, and if he ran across the doctor he would ask him to give him a look over.

Everyone in the club looked just the same as ever. He did not know why he should have expected them to look different. It was a comfort. These men, living for many years with one another lives that were methodically regulated, had acquired a number of little idiosyncrasies – one of them hummed incessantly while he played bridge, another insisted on drinking beer through a straw – and these tricks which had so often irritated the taipan now gave him a sense of security. He needed it, for he could not get out of his head that strange sight he had seen; he played bridge very badly; his partner was censorious, and the taipan lost his temper. He thought the men were looking at him oddly. He wondered what they saw in him that was unaccustomed.

Suddenly he felt he could not bear to stay in the club any longer. As he went out he saw the doctor reading *The Times* in the reading-room, but he could not bring himself to speak to him. He wanted to see for himself whether that grave was really there, and stepping into his chair he told his bearers to take him to the cemetery. You couldn't have a hallucination twice, could you? And besides, he would take the overseer in with him and if the grave was not there he wouldn't see it, and if it was he'd give the overseer the soundest thrashing he'd ever had. But the overseer was nowhere to be found. He had gone out and taken the keys with him. When the taipan found he could not get into the cemetery he felt suddenly exhausted. He got back into his chair and told his bearers to take him home. He would lie down for half an hour before dinner. He was tired out. That was it. He had heard that people had hallucinations when they were tired. When his boy came in to put out his clothes for dinner it was only by an effort of will that he got up. He had a strong inclination not to dress that evening, but he resisted it: he made it a rule to dress, he had dressed every evening for twenty years, and it would never do to break his rule. But he ordered a bottle of champagne with his dinner and that made him feel more comfortable. Afterwards he told the boy to bring him the best brandy. When he had drunk a couple of glasses of this he felt himself again. Hallucinations be damned! He went to the billiard-room and practised a few difficult shots. There could not be much the matter with him when his eye was so sure. When he went to bed he sank immediately into a sound sleep.

But suddenly he awoke. He had dreamed of that open grave and the coolies digging leisurely. He was sure he had seen them. It was absurd to say it was a hallucination when he had seen them with his own eyes. Then he heard the rattle of the night-watchman going his rounds. It broke upon the stillness of the night so harshly that it made him jump out of his skin. And then terror seized him. He felt a horror of the winding multitudinous streets of the Chinese city, and there was something ghastly and terrible in the convoluted roofs of the temples with their devils grimacing and tortured. He loathed the smells that assaulted his nostrils. And the people. Those myriads of blue-clad coolies, and the beggars in their filthy rags, and the merchants and the magistrates, sleek, smiling, and inscrutable, in their long black gowns. They seemed to press upon him with menace. He hated the country. China. Why had he ever come? He was panic-stricken now. He must get out. He would not stay another year, another month. What did he care about Shanghai?

'Oh, my God,' he cried, 'if I were only safely back in England.'

He wanted to go home. If he had to die he wanted to die in England. He could not bear to be buried among all these yellow men, with their slanting eyes and their grinning faces. He wanted to be buried at home, not in that grave he had seen that day. He could never rest there. Never. What did it matter what people thought? Let them think what they liked. The only thing that mattered was to get away while he had the chance.

He got out of bed and wrote to the head of the firm and said he had discovered he was dangerously ill. He must be replaced. He could not stay longer than was absolutely necessary. He must go home at once.

They found the letter in the morning clenched in the taipan's hand. He had slipped down between the desk and the chair. He was stone dead.

NOT YET SOLVED

Anonymous

The following is a true ghost story. It is an account of some supernatural incidents which have recently taken place in a clergyman's house situated in a favourite London suburb. They are so strange as to be thought worthy of publication, and are here given by one of the daughters of the house.

What I am about to relate is quite true in all the main facts, and I make the story known as being another of the many instances which prove that links undeniably exist between the spiritual and the material world.

There neither was nor is anything gloomy about the house. It became our home many years ago on account of it being the only available house to suit us near my father's church. When my father took the house it had been built about three years. During that time it was occupied by a Captain somebody (whose name I forget), his wife and little child, a girl. But the child had then died suddenly, it was said under very painful circumstances, and the parents were so distressed that they threw up the lease of the house and went away, and my father took it.

There was nothing gloomy, I have said, about the house. Neither was there any apparent reason why all of us children should shun a particular bedroom in it, which stood on the first landing, immediately over the dining-room, looking out into the street. It was a spacious, airy room, nothing whatever to be seen amiss with it; nevertheless, we little ones, from the eldest to the youngest, felt an unaccountable fear of it. It was in vain that our nurse and Aunt Jane, who, between them, supplied the place of the mother we had lost, strove to reassure us, saying there was nothing to fear. We did fear the room, and could not help it.

This unreasonable fear was, no doubt, augmented by one curious fact, which had been observed from the time we first entered the house. Constantly, and more especially during the spring and autumn time, the stone staircase, of which the first flight was composed, and which led on to the landing of the before-mentioned bedroom, seemed to be perpetually promenaded at night by small, pattering feet, as of a small child ceaselessly toiling up and down. Indeed, on our instalment in the house, Nurse, who had reason to suspect one of my brothers of the bad habit of walking in his sleep, would rise from her bed, and descend, candle in hand, with a warm shawl ready to wrap round the little sleep-walker.

The first time, not finding him, and thinking she had somehow missed him, she talked to him the next day, saying: 'He might catch his death of cold, stepping up and down them bare stone stairs.' The stairs were not carpeted, owing to a whim of my father's.

But soon, to her amazement, Nurse found the sounds were not caused by him; on each occasion she found him asleep in bed. But the pattering footsteps continued to be heard by all of us. After many conjectures as to the cause of the sounds, Aunt Jane and Nurse ceased to talk of them, at least, in our hearing, apparently paying them no attention. Indeed, in time we all grew accustomed to them, and never gave them much thought, except when visitors were staying in the house. The sounds disturbed them, and they would now and then make a remark on the restless nature of the young members of the household, 'who appeared to prefer walking up and down stairs at night to resting in bed'.

But to the bedroom we never did get reconciled. As we grew older, Aunt Jane reasoned with us, saying how very wrong it was to give way to superstition and fears, especially when the fears were groundless. To this day the sensation remains with us.

Thus the years went on.

One afternoon, as we were all gathered together for afternoon tea, a message was brought to Aunt Jane that a workman, then employed on the premises, wished to speak with her. Aunt Jane still stayed with us, notwithstanding my being now old enough to take my mother's place, as far as the housekeeping was concerned. The man was engaged in cleaning out a cistern at the extreme top of the house. 'What does he want with me?' asked Aunt Jane, but the servant did not know.

So Aunt Jane went out to him. On her return, she held a

very long, thin, and dirty-looking chain in her hand, which the workman had discovered in the cistern, it having, he said, in some extraordinary way, become wedged into a crack at one side, from which place he had extricated it. Aunt Jane rewarded the man for his honesty in bringing the chain to her; though whose it could possibly be and how it got there was an utter mystery. She thought the chain was gold.

My two brothers, both at the tea-table, pronounced the chain to be brass, and expressed their delight that Aunt Jane had been for once taken in, and had given five shillings for a worthless article. She strove to impress upon them that she had not given the man five shillings for the chain, which was none of his, but for his straightforward honesty.

Upon taking the chain to a jeweller's to be cleaned, we learned that it was a very fine Indian chain of pure gold, and of most delicate handicraft; which only served to increase the mystery of how it got into the place where it was found, and of how long it had lain there, hidden from the light of day.

When, a few days later, it was returned to us from the jeweller, glittering and clean, it was passed from one to another in wondering admiration, and shown to my father, who, until then, had only heard of its discovery, and had greatly pooh-poohed the idea of the chain being of any value.

'Found in the cistern at the top of the house!' he exclaimed, as we turned the beautiful thing about in our hands. 'That is most extraordinary!'

'I always said this was an uncanny house,' cried Ethel, the second of us, speaking upon impulse. 'All those unexplainable sounds of little footsteps for ever pattering up and down that stone staircase, and the curious feeling we have all had since we were little mites of shrinking from that front bedroom! It would not surprise me if a ghost were to turn up next.'

'Don't talk nonsense,' rebuked my father. 'We shall not keep a servant in the place if you begin to talk like that.'

'Well, at any rate,' went on the unabashed Ethel, 'how on earth did a fine long Indian chain, such as this, find its way into the top cistern?'

'That is the strange part of it,' said my brother Jack, who was minutely examining the chain. 'It is of value, this chain. What is to be done with it?'

'I shall wear it,' struck in Lily, the youngest of us, and

consequently the most indulged. 'I've just got a watch given to me, you know, and as I want a chain to wear with it, I'll take this one. If any owner claims it later, I can give it up to him.'

'The question is, to whom *does* it belong?' cried Jack. 'The man thought it had been in the crack of that cistern for years.'

Aunt Jane, struck by a thought, laid down her knitting – she was always knitting – and turned to my father, to speak.

'I should think it must have belonged to those people who lived in the house before you took it. The chain is an Indian chain; and they were said, were they not, to have come from India.'

'Yes, I believe so,' he replied, 'if my memory serves me correctly.'

'What did you hear about them?'

'Not much,' he answered. 'They had taken a long lease of the house, and had been in it about three years when their little girl died suddenly. After that, they gave up the lease, and I took it.'

'How did she die? What of?' asked Aunt Jane.

'I do not know. It was said that the circumstances attending the death were painful, and that the parents were so cut up at the loss they could not stay in the place. Their grief would naturally be great, she having been an only child. I think they went abroad,' added he. 'Anyway, that is all I recollect to have heard of them.'

Aunt Jane took up her knitting again. She thought the chain must have belonged to those people: and she wondered what it was that had caused the death of the little girl.

Lily was allowed to take the chain to wear; and our busy conjectures respecting it and its mysterious discovery gradually died away.

Shortly afterwards, a cousin of ours, from the country, took up his abode with us for a time, for the purpose of studying medicine, being intended for the medical profession. He was a jolly young Englishman, not much more than a lad, with an excellent appetite, and no imagination at all. As to any superstitious tale, had he been told one, he would have laughed it to pieces.

When a certain shyness, attendant on his first arrival, had worn off, Charley became a great addition to our circle, and his proverbial good temper soon made him a general favourite.

One bright spring morning, however, he appeared at breakfast in a different mood. After sitting some time in grumpy silence, he, to our amazement, burst out with a vehement attack on practical jokes.

What absurd folly such jokes were, he said, as if *he* could ever be taken in by them! 'So mind, Lena,' he went on, pouncing suddenly round on me, 'don't you try it on again. You know how I hate young kids of children!'

I asked him what he meant. The rest of them, sitting round, gazed at him, wondering what had come to good-humoured Charley.

'Because you may happen to have a child staying in the house, it's no reason why you girls should send it into my room in the night, just to play a trick on me.'

We assured him we had done nothing of the kind.

'You must have done so,' said Charley. 'Dressed it up in white, with its golden hair round its face. Whose child is it? One comfort, it must have caught a jolly cold, standing all that time looking at itself in the glass!'

'My dear Charley!' exclaimed I. 'What on earth are you talking about? There's no child staying here.'

'Oh, isn't there!' grumbled he; 'and you didn't send her into my room, thinking to startle me?'

'A little girl, you say?' – humouring him.

'A little girl about four years old, all in white, with lots of golden hair,' he repeated. 'As if you wanted to be told!'

'Charley, believe me: there's no little girl staying in the house; nor was one sent into your room.'

'I dare say not! Why, Lena, I lay awake full half an hour, watching her. She stood by the dressing-table, looking at something in her hand.'

'Did you see her come in?' I asked. I could not understand this at all. Charley was in desperate earnest.

'No, I didn't,' he answered. 'What roused me suddenly, I don't know; something did, and I sat up to look at my watch. It was just five o'clock; light enough for me to see everything in the room distinctly; and my eyes at once fell upon the child standing at the dressing-table.'

'Charley, you must have had a dream – or a nightmare.'

'I wish you'd not talk nonsense,' he angrily returned. 'I was as wide awake as I am now. Don't I tell you I watched the child for half an hour. When I got tired of sitting up in bed, I lay down and watched her. She was still there when I fell asleep.'

'Did you speak to her?'

'Not I!' cried Charley. 'I'd not give you girls the satisfaction you were no doubt all listening for, outside. If you weren't there yourselves, you had posted old Nurse there, I know.'

Nothing more was said then, for Charley had to hasten away to his daily work at the hospital. In fact, we got no more out of him on the subject at all. Our suggestion, that it was a dream, he would not listen to; and it took the whole household several days to convince him, or, perhaps, try to, that no child was or had been in the house.

Charley's bedroom was the uncanny room on the first landing, but we had never told him our dread of it. Not only that it would have been wrong to do so, but that we had grown a little ashamed of the feeling which yet we could not conquer.

It was, I think, about a year afterwards – and we had forgotten the occurrence – that the figure was seen again. One evening, when Lily and I, having lingered a little behind the others in saying goodnight, were preparing to mount to our particular nest at the top of the house, Ethel called me into her little room, saying she wanted to speak to me. It was next to the one Charles had slept in, and faced my brother's room at the other end of the long, straight landing. The gas was burning brightly on the staircase. Jack's door stood half-open, showing that his gas was also fully on. I went into Ethel's room, Lily waiting for me outside; but a minute had hardly elapsed ere she called out quickly, in a low, sharp voice:

'Come here, Lena; make haste!'

I was reading a letter Ethel had just put into my hand, so I answered shortly: 'In a minute!'

'Make haste!' she cried again. 'Be quick!'

I ran out, rather impatiently, to find Lily gazing hard at Jack's door, with a strange, fixed look in her eyes.

'I have just seen the little girl Charles saw,' she said, solemnly. 'She was looking straight at me, dressed all in white, and she had such lovely golden hair! When you came, she vanished.'

Nothing was to be seen then. We looked around, no one stirring. Ethel had joined us.

'Lily,' spoke Ethel, presently, 'perhaps she was looking at the gold chain: you have it on.'

The chain was quite conspicuous outside Lily's dress. She repeated again that the little girl had stood gazing at her. Charles, we remembered, had said she did not look at him, but was all the time looking apparently at something in her hand. Lily had not felt any fear. The golden hair, she declared, was perfectly beautiful.

'This is really very strange,' exclaimed Aunt Jane, who, hearing our voices, had appeared on the scene to know what the talking was about. 'Are you quite sure, Lily, of what you say?'

'Of course I am sure,' returned Lily, who never could bear to be doubted, and was very matter-of-fact and truthful. 'The little girl stood there gazing at me, Aunt. She was as plainly to be seen as we are to one another.'

'We were wondering, Aunt, whether she could be looking at the chain which Lily has on,' said Ethel. 'Perhaps she recognized it? You know, when the chain was found, we thought it might possibly have belonged to the people who were in the house before us.' Which, of course, as Aunt Jane observed, was as much as to suggest that this little girl with the mass of golden hair might be the apparition of the child who had died in the house.

We talked of it as the days went on, suggesting all kinds of possibilities and impossibilities. As she had never appeared until after the discovery of the chain, we could but think the chain might in some way or other be connected with her, and that, if the chain had, indeed, belonged to the first occupiers of the house, the little spirit might well be that of the child who had died there. Another question we asked ourselves was: Could the chain, or its loss, have had aught to do with her death?

The story spread, and people came to see the room and passage where the little figure had appeared; but it was some time before it was seen again. Lily was married. She had left home and taken the chain with her.

Ethel was climbing slowly up the stone staircase one Sunday evening between seven and eight o'clock, when she saw the little white figure, crowned with its mass of golden curls, peeping through the banisters on the first landing, within three yards of her. It was a cold winter evening, and the gas was burning as usual on the staircase. The passages were always kept very bright. Ethel paused, and the little figure turned its head towards her, and then vanished. It was almost as though she had been looking out for someone, but not Ethel. Ethel, like Lily, felt no fear or surprise at the time. She noticed particularly the gloriously bright golden hair.

This last appearance was seen but a few months back, and it has revived all our curiosity, wonder and interest. Whether we shall ever learn the truth concerning the little dead maiden, and whether the gold chain is in any way connected with her mysterious visits, must remain for the present a mystery.

INTO THE MAD, MAD WORLD

Terry Tapp

Another year has drifted by and Rachel, once again, sits on a chair which has been thoughtfully bolted to the floor. The corridor echoes to clinical steel footsteps as stone-faced nurses march grimly about their business and Rachel waits and smiles.

She knows, deep in her heart, that she should not be in this place at all, yet she cannot convince them that she is telling the truth. Everything she tells them is true . . . and they will not believe her. How simple it would be to fool them; how easy it would be to admit that it was all a figment of her imagination. Rachel smiles again with secret amusement as she imagines the satisfied look on the face of the visiting psychiatrist as he signs her file and scribbles the words on the outside, 'Recommended for Release'. The walnut-grained door swishes open and an elderly man is beckoning Rachel's nurse.

'We will see Bowden now,' he tells the nurse as if Rachel herself was not there. The words are spat out, like annoying pips. 'We will see Bowden now.' Bowden . . . everyone is addressed by surname . . . surname . . . surname . . .

It had been a lovely day; at least, it had been normal. Robin had telephoned to say that he was on his way home and Mark, like all three-year-olds, had been a tyrant. He had broken a cup, spilled flour over the kitchen floor and pulled the electric kettle from the kitchen unit. Thank God it had been empty. Or should God be thanked? What if that kettle had been full of steaming, scalding water? Should God be thanked?

About six-thirty she had tucked young Mark gratefully into his bed, kissed him good night and marvelled how a bath and change of clothing could transform a bad-tempered tyrant into an angelic-faced, cuddly boy. Funny that, how children change at bedtime. So rosy-faced, so happy and . . . and blue-eyed. Those eyes. Were they really that colour? How deep and blue, like icy sapphires, like oceans and skies. Eyes so blue they had a depth and vividness that was almost painful to behold.

How she had chided herself for being so short-tempered with him during the day. She had kissed him warmly, luxuriating in the feel of his warm young hands as they slid around her neck and squeezed her lovingly. 'Good night, Mummy,' Mark had said. 'Sleepy tight.'

'Mind the bed bugs don't bite,' she had replied absently, as she always did. Bedtime was a ritual of such nonsensical things . . . nonsensical but very dear to both of them. Tucking in the bedclothes, she had stroked back his straw-coloured hair to reveal those piercing eyes of blue, all the frustrations of the day evaporating in the heat of her love for him. And Mark had gazed at her with adoring eyes, a sleepy smile dissolving from his face as he fell back into the warm and open arms of sleep.

She had crept to the door thinking that tomorrow would be different. Tomorrow she would be more patient with him. After all, he was only a child . . . child . . . child . . .

'Come along, Bowden. Don't dawdle in the doorway.' The starchy nurse is rasping harshly in her ear and Rachel feels fingers of cruel steel wire dig into the soft flesh of her upper arm. Angrily she tears herself out of the grasp, the nails gouging deeply into her arm, making her cry aloud with the pain of it.

'There is no need to be so brutal,' she is telling the granite-faced nurse. 'I am not an animal, you know.'

'Then pay attention when I speak to you, Bowden,' the nurse is pouting and pushing at Rachel's back.

Rachel walks to the open door, taps gently on the rich grained pattern and steps into the office. It is warm in the office and the carpet is thick, maybe thicker even than the one in Rachel's lounge. Rachel's lounge? 'Do I have a lounge?' she is thinking. 'Does the house still half belong to me?'

'Come in, Bowden,' the voice issues from the folds of a weak mouth that opens and shuts like a gaping goldfish in a tank. The goldfish man, bald-headed and sweating, does not bother to look up at her and continues to scribble on the file. He has no manners, not even bothering to get up from his chair when a lady enters the room. He is scowling at the file of papers and points his newly sharpened pencil to a hard chair, absently indicating that he wants to see Rachel obediently sitting on it when he finally condescends to look up at her.

He is muttering to himself, unaware that the other two men in the office are exchanging significant glances, and he finally puts a full stop on to the file as if he has just created the world. All that waiting and all that play acting for one full stop. Slowly his eyes are lifting towards the chair. He notices that there are no human legs near the chair and his eyes dart about the room swiftly, then settle on Rachel's legs, making her squirm with displeasure as the eyes grope up her body to her face.

Again the pencil is pointed to the chair and a look of surprised displeasure darkens the weak face. Rachel is staring at him defiantly. She knows he wants her to sit on the chair, but why should he be allowed to display such bad manners? It costs nothing to smile, to greet a person civilly and enquire if one would like to be seated.

Having made his point, the man returns to his file, no doubt to spend another precious minute searching for a place to insert yet another of those pompous full stops. How ill-mannered! Rachel is determined not to sit until she has been invited properly and she is staring at the door . . . door . . . door . . .

She had stood at the door, listening to the even breathing of her son, thinking how patient she would be in future. Then she had taken one last loving look at him and crept from the room, unaware that she would never, ever, be allowed the privilege of putting her son to bed again.

She had walked out on to the landing, gently closed the door and turned towards the wide staircase. She had walked out on to the landing, gently closed the door and turned towards the wide staircase. She had . . . But what was the use of going over and over the same ground again? It had been the last, the very last action that she remembered before her world had erupted.

She had gently closed the door, her heart brimful of love

for young Mark, eagerly looking forward to the return of her husband. Then she had slowly turned towards the wide staircase.

Smoke. That had been her first thought. Maybe something had caught fire. The dinner! It would be ruined. She had started to run downstairs when something made her stop instantly.

There had been a face in the smoke. A vague, ethereal face, so hideous, so old and so very evil.

Stuff and nonsense! she had told herself, her eyes searching the shifting vapours for another glimpse of the face. Again she had tried to dismiss the image from her mind as a cold draught of air enfolded her. She had been frozen by that air. It was cold, yet not the fresh and frosty cold of a winter's morning; it had been a deathly, sick and clammy cold that makes the body ill and feverish.

And the face solidified into a recognizable shape again. What rubbish! It must be an illusion . . . illusion . . . illusion . . .

'Sit down, Bowden,' a voice is snapping and crackling at her. Rachel smiles, realizing that the bald-headed man has, at last, given up the attempt to intimidate her. Now he will try to get his own back by behaving badly.

She is not moving, her face just catches the sun as she smiles at the bald-headed man and waits for an invitation rather than a command. It could take all day, but what does she care? She has all day to waste . . . all day . . . all week.

'Will you *please* sit down,' she corrects him stonily. 'I may be what you term a patient in this institution, but even patients have the privilege of being human beings. It is certainly not an excuse for you to be so abrupt and ill-mannered.'

Perfect. The other two men silently and mirthfully applaud her and the bald-headed man is grinning sickly yellow, displaying his stained teeth and coated tongue. His smile turns to one of amused tolerance as he attempts to embrace his colleagues with a reassuring grin. He fails and is fiddling busily with papers on his desk, thinking what to say next.

'Would you please sit down . . . Bowden.' The words fall from wet lips and are loaded with malice, his face is grey with anger and he stares at Rachel, his fingers drumming a menacing tattoo, his eyes narrowed and loathing . . . evil . . . hateful eyes that drill and probe and search. Rachel is staring at him, determined not to give way. She stares at those eyes . . . eyes . . . eyes . . .

The eyes had been evil. As the smoke had solidified, she had first noticed the eyes. Hot, volcanic eyes that had scorched and burned their way into the memory, blotting out all other terrible memories with horrific clarity. Those eyes had held her like a speared-through bird, fluttering and panting, yet unable to move.

'Stuff and nonsense,' she had cried aloud, partly to comfort herself as does a person who whistles in the darkness. 'There must be an explanation.'

'Is there?' The voice had not surprised her, for she had lived the last few seconds in dread that the apparition might see her and try to speak. But the words came out of the shifting vapour and had chilled her heart, freezing it mid-beat and leaving her with a salty metallic taste in her mouth.

She had not replied to the voice, preferring instead to ignore it, run downstairs and seek the familiarity and sanctuary of her busy kitchen. She had always thought that the house had an air of evil about it, but Robin with his prim and sensible ways had dissuaded her from that opinion. She decided to go . . . to run downstairs while she had the chance . . . for if this thing, this ghost or whatever it was, should try to speak again, she would not be able to stop the naked, raw-edged scream that bubbled up in her throat.

'You are afraid,' the voice had taunted. 'You look at the floor and you stare at the ceiling and you are too afraid to look at me.'

'I am *not* afraid,' Rachel had cried aloud, hoping to frighten the thing with her new authority.

'You spoke! You spoke to me!' the apparition cackled. 'Unless you are insane, and I am perfectly sure you are not, you have admitted that I exist!'

And she had.

She knew, by the very fact that she was protesting, that she *had* seen that dreadful thing. Her mind was in a state of suspension, holding the image behind a frosted glass, unable to allow her brain to see it fully.

'I do not admit it,' she had yelled with all her might, knowing that each outburst was solidifying the image, making it more and more a reality. 'I do not admit it! I do not admit it . . . admit it . . . admit it . . .'

Still the bald-headed man stares at her, but he is weakening and Rachel is determined that she will hold on. Why should he be allowed to try to outstare her? What victory will he gain? He will not outstare her though . . . she will not permit it.

'My name is Regan,' the bald-headed man is telling her, his eyes still fixed on her as if he is hypnotized. 'You know Doctor Rogers and the other gentleman is Doctor Harper.'

Harper is nodding like one of those loose-headed dogs that grin inanely from the backs of cars and Dr Rogers is just stuffing black tobacco into his gnarled pipe, trying to display the utmost confidence in Rachel's ability to pass the scrutiny of this panel. But Rachel knows that he winks at her to comfort himself, not because he really has confidence in her.

'You are aware,' Regan has shifted his eyes away from her . . . defeated. 'You are aware that this panel has the authority to release, or detain you as they see fit?'

This is the snag. This is the threat.

Yes, of course she knows of his power. Regan does not have to remind her and she knows that he will be very demanding anyway. Regan cannot afford to make mistakes . . . he has already made one too many by releasing a man last month. That man raped and stabbed a young woman within hours of his release . . . a release granted by Regan. Oh, no; Regan will not make another mistake. He will not allow anything to pass his eagle, shifting eyes.

'This is, as you must be aware, another opportunity to convince us that you are a fit person to resume your life in the society of normal people.' Regan holds the pencil at eye level, staring over it, flexing it as he meets Rachel's cool gaze. 'We have had an opportunity to study the psychiatrist's reports on you and now we will have to establish your own position.'

There is a silence. Regan is staring at Rachel, waiting for her to respond to his remarks. Dr Harper is still nodding his head, agreeable with everything and anything. Is she sane? That's good then. She's mad? Poor girl. What difference does it make to men like Dr Harper? He nods his agreement for everything. More steamed pudding? He nods. Nice day? He nods. God, how stupid he looks just nodding and smiling away.

'Have a cigarette, Rachel,' Dr Rogers is standing by her, a cigarette now dangling from his lips. He is smiling nervously and Rachel knows that he goes through it every time she is interviewed. Dr Rogers gets the nerves while she gets another year's detention . . . and another year . . . and another. Dr Rogers even had a sympathetic pregnancy when she was expecting Mark. Dr Rogers would never, ever, admit it, but he is in love with Rachel. His fingers are shaking as he struggles with the obstinate lighter and Rachel feels like giggling. It's like when she was young and gangling youths nervously tried to impress her with gulping, awkward, nervous actions.

Dr Rogers has lighted the cigarette and is pushing an ash-tray over to Rachel as he sits down again. The ashtray, unlike the ones elsewhere in the building, is not screwed down. She smiles and picks the ashtray up, weighing it in her hand and causing a look of alarm to show itself on Regan's face. How dearly she would love to smash this tray . . . and smash it into Regan's face. Glass and bone . . . blood, glass and bone!

Regan appears to read her thoughts and is framing his next speech. He wants to be seen to be fair, but Rachel knows that he has already made up his mind.

'Before we can release you, Bowden,' Regan continues, 'we must be one hundred per cent sure about you. We have been seeking some improvement in your attitude. Some indication of your awareness of other people. You have spent a long time here and we certainly have no desire to detain you longer than is necessary.'

Rachel is fascinated by the way Regan's lips move, the small bead of saliva being stretched and loosened like an elastic band. She wonders when it will break, but it does not. The saliva moves and stretches as the lips contort in an ungainly water ballet. She smells foul breath and sees the grinning malicious mouth that mocks and dribbles . . . dribbles . . . dribbles . . .

'You are trying to fight it,' the voice had cackled. The smoke had been transformed into a definite shape and she had watched it, biting her lip hard.

'You see me and you feel, me, Rachel, yet you try to deny it. Your eyes see me and you know I am real.'

She had clamped her eyes shut, willing herself to come up, up out of this dreadful nightmare. But it was actually happening. Even through closed eyelids, she had seen that awful, hideous face.

'Ghosts *are* real,' the old man had cried (for he was in the shape of a very old man), his face alive with wrinkles, his eyes asmoke with malice.

'Who – who are you?' She had asked the question automatically, realizing that a name would not make the dreadful thing less fearsome.

'I am no one . . . yet,' the old man had laughed. 'You see, child, ghosts are not the disembodied spirits of those who have been. Oh no! Ghosts are empty, restless spirits who wait their time to take possession of a body.'

'But I see you as an old man,' she had objected, still keeping her eyes on the stairs where she had intended to make a run for it.

'You see me as an old man,' the apparition had replied. 'I think you see me as an old and *ugly* man because you are afraid of me. Others, those who are not afraid, will see me as other things.'

'What do you want with us?' she had asked.

'Nothing – nothing with you, my dear,' the old man had croaked. 'It is your son I have come to see.'

'Mark?' The twanging steel strings of her nerves had snapped, lashing back with cutting fury. 'What do you want him for? He's only a child!'

'A child of three. A three-year-old child is of the age . . .'

Of the age . . . Mark was of the age to be possessed? It hadn't sounded true at the time. How could the old man possess a baby of three? How could he? Could he . . . could he . . . ?

Regan is staring at Rachel as she grinds the cigarette into the glass ashtray. She grinds it hard, killing the fiery red-hot end with her bare fingers. Harder and harder . . . grind the cigarette hard until the pain screams up the fingers and makes the brain ice cold and calculating. Grind it into the glass and pretend it's Regan's face. The pain cuts wide open wounds, purifies and refreshes.

Obviously Regan has noted the incident. People often inflict injury upon themselves when they are mentally disturbed. Regan is smiling a triumphant smile, the pencil flexing glossily between his stubby fingers. He beams and sweats his victory as the pencil bows . . . then snaps.

'I want you to listen to me carefully, Bowden,' he is saying. He sounds like a man on a talent contest, introducing an act that doesn't really have a chance, but he wants to be seen to be scrupulously fair . . . even though he is cheating. 'You see, Bowden, we don't want to keep you locked in here just because you suffer from hallucinations. Good God, we aren't monsters! But the danger for a patient such as yourself, is when you actually believe that the hallucination is real. Now, if you can honestly tell us, and mean it sincerely, that you do not believe that the hallucinations you saw were real . . . well, I think we will be able to let you out of here for Christmas. Wouldn't that be nice? You could go home to your family – ' Regan is scanning the file to see that she does have a family – 'Yes, you have a son and a fine husband I see.'

'Does it say that there?' Rachel interrupts. 'I mean, does it say that I have a fine husband? Does it actually say fine?'

Regan knows that it does not say 'fine' husband. He is really doing his best to be pleasant.

'I hope you realize that you are not progressing your release,' Regan is snapping, the saliva is still stretching like a rubber band. 'We have the power to detain you here as long as we see fit.'

'We have the power . . . the power . . . power . . .'

That's what the old man had said. He had chuckled as Rachel had run across the landing to bar his way to Mark's bedroom.

'You will not get in here!' she had cried. 'I won't let you!'

'I have the power to *be* in there,' the evil face had leered. 'I have the power to inhabit the body of my choice and there is no power that can deny me that right.'

'But why Mark? Why must you use him?'

'He is but a body.' The reply had been casual. 'He serves the purpose until he reaches his middle age. After that time, I will free myself of him and find another body . . . another temple for my soul.'

Then he had conjured up the fire, making it appear as if the whole house were burning. He had conjured wicked, roaring lions before her eyes, exploring every crevice of her fears and toying with her as a cat toys with a mouse. Spiders, hairy and poisonous creatures with spastic, lethal movements that had made her shudder; rats, snakes, bats . . . blood. Yet she did not let the thing pass her. Nothing would get into Mark's bedroom while she still lived!

The eyes had glowed hot; molten eyes that burned and blasted out a heat . . . a shrivelling heat that melted courage like butter.

God! She would never forget those scarlet, fiery eyes. Evil eyes that laughed, raped, scorched and screamed unspeakable obscenities into her mind. Hypnotic eyes that drilled and probed into the skull.

She had opened her eyes . . . and it was gone.

It was gone! Gone! Gone!

'Our power is quite final, Bowden,' Regan is still chanting out his rights. He wants to justify himself to her, to the other two men. He wants to reassure himself that he is doing the right thing . . . and Rachel doesn't give a damn.

'Your husband is waiting outside in the interview room. He wants you back home again.' Dr Rogers is speaking; he is leaning forward earnestly, his face furrowed with lines of concern for her. 'Your son, Mark . . . he's a fine lad now. Why don't you break your rule, Rachel? You go out there and talk to them. You know, I'm sure it would be the turning point in your life if only you would make the effort. Why, you wouldn't credit what a fine lad young Mark is, and your husband, he's been so loyal over the years. He still calls every week, even though you refuse to see him when he gets here.'

Rachel is thinking. What if she did go out and see them? What if she just perked herself up and went out there and sat down like nothing had happened at all? Could she just pick up the threads? It would be easy . . . oh, so very easy just to agree with this man Regan. Even now she still has a chance. All she has to do is tell Regan that she is ashamed of her bad manners. Of course it was all a nervous breakdown, and that's what has caused these hallucinations. So easy . . . so very, very easy. Then she could go back to her home and pick up the threads. Mark would never be the baby he once was and things would be strange at first. She would have to explain things to the neighbours . . . maybe Robin would agree to shifting houses? But would he ever forget? Forget? Forget?

What a relief it had been when the old man had just vanished like that. What a blessed relief when he had shown his fury and just vanished. Never again would she doubt that there were such things as ghosts.

She had sighed her relief and opened the door to see that Mark had not been awakened by the noises . . . and then she knew.

Baby Mark was thrashing in his bed, his eyes were bulging sacs of blue as he struggled at his throat. He writhed and jerked in epileptic convulsions, his whole body lifting at times from the bed.

'Dear God!' Rachel had screamed. 'You won't get into him. By all the saints I abjure thee, Satan! I defy thee!' A bible . . . prayer book . . . anything sacred! The baby chokes and vomits as the spirit enters his body.

'You will not possess him!' Rachel had screamed, grasping the pillow in her hands. 'I'd rather he died than . . . than . . .'

And having made the decision, she had put the pillow over her son's face . . . pressing . . . pressing . . . pressing.

'What in God's name!' Robin had rushed up to the bedroom. He had still been carrying his briefcase and he stared at his wife as she had pushed violently down on the pillow.

'For Christ's sake, Rachel!'

'But you don't understand. He is evil . . . he is evil!'

No time to explain . . . they had fought and scratched each other while Mark lay writhing in his bed, his eyes starting out of their sockets. Of course, Rachel had lost the fight, but then, she was used to that. Used to losing . . . losing . . . losing . . .

'Would you like to see your husband?' Dr Rogers is speaking firmly, his face anxious and white.

Dear God, the years had not quenched the love she felt for Robin. Of course she wanted to see him . . . but dare she? She doesn't want to see that face . . . that lovely face of his shows all the disappointment. She knows she is not a pretty sight at the moment. What reason has there been to take care of herself? The dress is stiff and drab and grey. Her hair is cropped and she may wear no make-up without permission.

'May I see them?' The words are out of her mouth before she realizes it. Her heart leaps as she makes the decision and she instantly wonders what Mark will look like after all these years. Will he have forgiven her? Will Robin still love her?

'We will wait for you here,' Regan is lighting a cigarette.

'This way, Bowden.' The steel fingers grip her arm again and this time Rachel rejoices in the pain. Pain is reality and the reality is that she is going to see her son and her husband.

They walk from the room together, walk down the corridor and out into the big room with the wire-netting screen and the screwed-down chairs. Robin turns and sees his wife and Rachel is praying deep down inside herself. 'Dear God,' she keeps mumbling. 'Dear God, you know what I want. You know . . .'

And Robin smiles and there is love between them. Mark turns and smiles, his face almost unchanged from that of babyhood. Firm jaw, blond hair . . . but the *eyes*! Those eyes are molten volcanoes . . . smouldering and smoking out with fetid evil. He laughs . . . a loud, evil laugh!

'Get them out of here!' Rachel leaps at the netting, her face twisted into a snarl. 'Get those two bastards out of here!'

Robin starts back in fear; his eyes tell her that he will never cease to be afraid of her.

And Mark is serious-faced . . . yet his eyes mock and jeer at her.

'Come along, Bowden,' the nurse flexes her steel fingers around Rachel's arm. 'Come along, Bowden, or I'll have to give you the treatment. I'll get the water!'

She is dragged screaming out of the room and her cries

echo down the long corridor as she sobs and giggles and moans.

Regan watches her being dragged along and closes the file tight like a shark's jaw.

'I don't ever want to leave here,' Rachel is screaming. 'I couldn't bear it if you sent me out there. I don't want to go out into that mad, mad place!'

And Rachel is still screaming . . .

THE HOSTELRY

Guy de Maupassant

At the foot of the glaciers, in those naked and rock-bound *couloirs* which indent the snow-clad ranges of the High Alps, you will find every here and there a guest-house. These little hostelries are constructed of timber and are all built very much to the same pattern. The Schwarenbach Inn was one of them.

The Schwarenbach served as a refuge to travellers attempting the passage of the Gemmi. For the six summer months it remained open, with Jean Hauser's family in residence; but as soon as the early snows began to accumulate, filling the valley and rendering the descent to Loeche impracticable, Jean Hauser with his three sons and his wife and daughter quitted the house, leaving it in charge of the old guide Gaspard Hari and his companion, together with Sam, the big mountain-bred dog. The two men, with the dog, lived in their prison of snow until the spring arrived. They had nothing to look at, except the vast white slopes of the Balmhorn. Pale glistening mountain peaks rose all round them. They were shut in, blockaded, by the snow; it lay on them like a shroud, growing ever deeper and deeper until the little house was enveloped, closed in, obliterated. The snow piled itself upon the roof, blinded the windows and walled up the door.

On the day on which the Hauser family took their departure for Loeche, the winter was close at hand, and the descent was becoming dangerous. The three sons set off on foot leading three mules laden with household belongings. Behind them followed the mother, Jeanne Hauser, and her daughter Louise, both riding the same mule. Next and last came the father and the two caretakers. The latter were to accompany the family as far as the beginning of the track that leads down the mountain-side to Loeche.

The party first skirted the edge of the little lake, already frozen, in its rocky hollow in front of the inn; then they proceeded along the valley, which lay before them, a white sheet of snow, with icy peaks dominating it on every side.

A flood of sunshine fell across the whiteness of this frozen wilderness, lighting it up with a cold, blinding brilliance. There was no sign of life in this sea of mountains; not a movement could be seen in the limitless solitude; not a sound disturbed the profound silence.

Gradually the younger of the guides, Ulrich Kunsi, a tall long-limbed Swiss, forged ahead of the two older men and overtook the mule on which the two women were riding. The daughter saw him as he approached and there was sadness in the glance with which she summoned him to her side.

She was a little peasant girl with a complexion like milk. Her flaxen hair was so pale that one would fancy it had been bleached by prolonged residence amongst the snows and glaciers.

On overtaking the mule on which Louise and her mother were riding, Ulrich Kunsi placed his hand on the crupper and slackened his pace. The mother began talking; she expounded in infinite detail her instructions for wintering. It was the first time that Ulrich had stayed behind. Old Hari, on the other hand, had already accomplished his fourteenth hibernation, under the snow that covered the Schwarenbach Inn.

Ulrich listened, but without any appearance of grasping what was said. He never took his eyes off the daughter. Every now and then he would reply: 'Yes, Madame Hauser.' But his thoughts seemed far away, and his face remained calm and impassive.

They reached the Daubensee, which lies at the foot of the valley. Its surface was now a vast level sheet of ice. On the right, the rocks of the Daubenhorn, dark and precipitous, rose above the vast moraines of the Lemmern Glacier, and the Wildstrubel towered over all.

As they approached the Gemmi saddle, from which begins the descent to Loeche, they suddenly beheld, across the deep wide valley of the Rhone, the prodigious sky-line of the Valais Alps, a distant multitude of white peaks of unequal size, some pointed, some flattened, but all glistening in the rays of the sun.

There was the two-horned Mischabel, the majestic mass of the Weisshorn, the lumbering Brunegghorn, the lofty and fear-inspiring Cervin, which has killed so many men, and the Dent-Blanche, monstrous yet alluring. Below them, in an enormous hollow at the foot of terrifying precipices, they caught sight of Loeche, so far away from them that the houses seemed like a handful of sand, thrown down into the vast crevasse which has at one end the barrier of the Gemmi, and at the other a wide exit to the Rhone valley.

They had reached the head of a path, which winds downwards in serpentine coils, fantastic and extraordinary, along the mountain-side, until it reaches the almost invisible village at the foot. The mule stopped and the two women jumped down into the snow. By this time the two older men had overtaken the rest of the party.

'Now, friends,' said old Hauser, 'we must say goodbye till next year. And keep your hearts up.'

'Till next year,' replied Hari.

The men embraced. Madame Hauser gave her cheek to be kissed and her daughter followed her example. When it was Ulrich Kunsi's turn to kiss Louise, he whispered in her ear:

'Don't forget us up on our heights.'

'No,' she replied in tones so low that he guessed, rather than heard, the word.

'Well, well, goodbye,' said old Hauser again. 'Take care of yourselves.'

He strode on past the women and led the way downwards. All three were lost to view at the first bend in the track. Gaspard and Ulrich turned back towards the Schwarenbach Inn. They walked slowly and in silence, side by side. They had seen the last of their friends. They were to be alone, with no other companionship, for four or five months.

Gaspard Hari began to tell Ulrich about the previous winter. His companion then had been Michael Carol; but accidents were likely to happen during the long solitude, and Michael had grown too old for the job. Still, they had had a pretty good time together. The secret of the whole thing was to make up your mind to it from the beginning. Sooner or later one invented distractions and games and things to while away the time.

With downcast eyes Ulrich Kunsi listened to his companion, but his thoughts were following the women, who were making their way to the village, down the zigzag path on the Gemmi mountain-side.

They soon caught sight of the distant inn. It looked very tiny, like a black dot at the base of the stupendous mountain of snow. When they opened the door of the house, Sam, the great curly-haired dog, gambolled round them joyfully.

'Well, Ulrich, my boy,' said old Gaspard, 'we have no women here now. We must get dinner ready ourselves. You can set to and peel the potatoes.'

They sat down on wooden stools and began to prepare the soup. The forenoon of the following day seemed long to Ulrich Kunsi. Old Hari smoked his pipe and spat into the fireplace. The younger man looked through the window at the superb mountain, which rose in front of the house. In the afternoon he went out, and pursuing the road he had taken the previous day, he followed the tracks of the mule on which the two women had ridden. He arrived at last at the saddle of the Gemmi, and lying prone on the edge of the precipice, gazed down on Loeche. The village, nestling in its rocky hollow, had not yet been obliterated by the snow. But there was snow very near it. Its advance had been arrested by the pine forests which guarded the environs of the hamlet. Seen from a height, the low houses of the village looked like paving-stones set in a field.

Ulrich reflected that Louise Hauser was now in one of those grey cottages. Which one was it, he wondered. They were too remote to be separately distinguished. He had a yearning to go down there while it was still possible. But the sun had disappeared behind the great peak of Wildstrubel, and Ulrich turned homewards. He found Hari smoking. On Ulrich's return Hari proposed a game of cards and the two men sat down on opposite sides of the table. They played for a long time at a simple game called brisque. Then they had supper and went to bed.

Subsequent days were like the first, clear and cold, without any fresh fall of snow. Gaspard passed his days watching the eagles and other rare birds, which adventure themselves in these frozen altitudes. For his part, Ulrich went regularly to the *col* to look down at the distant village. In the evening they played cards, dice and dominoes, staking small objects to lend an interest to the game.

One morning, Hari, who had been the first to rise, called

out to Ulrich. A drifting cloud of white foam, deep yet ethereal, was sinking down on them and on all around them, spreading over them slowly, silently, a cover which grew ever thicker and heavier. The snowfall lasted four days and four nights. The door and windows had to be cleared, a passage dug, and steps cut, to enable them to climb out on to the surface of powdery snow, which twelve hours of frost had made harder than the granite of the moraines.

After that, they lived as in a prison, hardly ever venturing outside their dwelling. The household tasks were divided between them and were punctually performed. Ulrich Kunsi undertook the cleaning and washing up and keeping the house neat. He also split the firewood. Hari kept the fire going and did the cooking. These necessary and monotonous tasks were relieved by long contests at dice or cards. Being both of them of calm and placid temperament, they never quarrelled. They never went even as far as to display impatience or peevishness, or to speak sharply to each other, both having determined beforehand to make the best of their wintry sojourn on the heights. Occasionally Gaspard took his gun and went out hunting chamois, and when he had the good luck to kill one, it was high day and holiday in the Schwarenbach Inn and there was great feasting on fresh meat.

One morning Hari set forth on one of these expeditions. The thermometer outside the inn showed thirty degrees of frost. Hari started before sunrise, hoping to take the chamois by surprise on the lower slopes of the Wildstrubel.

Left to himself, Ulrich remained in bed until ten o'clock. He was by nature a good sleeper, but he would not have dared to give way to this proclivity in the presence of the old guide, who was an early riser and always full of energy. He lingered over his breakfast, which he shared with Sam, who passed his days and nights sleeping in front of the fire. After breakfast he felt his spirits oppressed, and almost daunted, by the solitude, and he longed for his daily game of cards with the unconquerable craving that comes of ingrained habit. Later, he went out to meet his comrade, who was due to return at four o'clock.

The whole valley was now of a uniform level under its thick covering of snow. The crevasses were full to the top;

the two lakes could no longer be distinguished; the rocks lay hid under a snowy quilt. Lying at the foot of the immense peaks, the valley was now one immense basin, symmetrical, frozen, and of a blinding whiteness.

It was three weeks since Ulrich had been to the edge of the precipice from which he looked down at the village. He thought he would go there again, before climbing the slopes that led to the Wildstrubel. The snow had now reached Loeche, and the houses were lost under their white mantle.

Turning to the right, he reached the Lemmern glacier. He walked with the mountaineer's long stride, driving his iron-pointed stick down on to the snow, which was as hard as stone. With his far-sighted eyes he sought the small black dot which he expected to see moving, in the far distance, over this vast sheet of snow. On reaching the edge of the glacier he stopped, wondering whether old Hari had really come that way. Then, with increasing anxiety and quicker steps, he began to skirt the moraines.

The sun was sinking. The snow was suffused with a tinge of pink, and over its crystalline surface swept sharp gusts of a dry and icy breeze. Ulrich tried to reach his friend with a call, shrill, vibrant, prolonged. His voice took its flight into the deathless silence, in which the mountains slept. It rang far out over the deep motionless undulations of frozen foam, like the cry of a bird over the waves of the sea. Then it died away. And there was no reply.

He walked on and on. The sun had sunk behind the peaks, and the purple glow of sunset still lingered about them, but the depths of the valley were grey and shadowy, and Ulrich was suddenly afraid. He had an idea that the silence, the cold, the solitude were taking possession of him, were about to arrest his circulation and freeze his blood, stiffen his limbs and convert him into a motionless, frozen image. With all speed he could, he ran back towards the Inn. Hari, he thought, must have taken another way and reached home already. He would find him seated by the fire, with a dead chamois at his feet. He soon came in sight of the hostelry. There was no smoke issuing from the chimney. Ulrich ran yet faster, and when he opened the door of the house, Sam leaped up to greet him. But there was no Gaspard Hari.

In consternation Kunsi turned hither and thither, as though expecting to find his comrade hiding in a corner. Then he relighted the fire and made the soup, still hoping that he would look up and see the old man coming in. From time to time he went outside, in case there should be some sign of him. Night had fallen, that wan, livid night of the mountains, illumined only by the slender, yellow crescent of a new moon, which was sinking towards the skyline and would soon disappear behind the ridge.

Returning to the house, Ulrich sat down by the fire and while he was warming his hands and feet, his thoughts ran on possible accidents. Gaspard might have broken a leg, or fallen into a hollow, or made a false step, which had cost him a sprained ankle. He would be lying in the snow, helpless against the benumbing cold, in agony of mind, far from any other human soul, calling out for help, shouting with all the strength of his voice in the silence of the night.

How to discover where he was? So vast and craggy was the mountain, so dangerous the approaches to it, especially in the winter, that it would take ten or twenty guides searching for a week in all directions to find a man in that immensity. None the less Ulrich made up his mind to take Sam and set forth to look for Gaspard, if he had not come back by one in the morning.

He made his preparations. He put two days' provisions into a bag, took his cramp-irons, wound round his waist a long, strong, slender rope, and inspected thoroughly his spiked stick and his ice-axes. Then he waited. The fire was burning with a clear flame; the great dog lay snoring in its warmth; the steady ticking of the clock, in its resonant wooden case, sounded like the beating of a heart. Still he waited, his ears straining to catch any distant noise. When the light breeze whispered round roof and walls, he shivered.

The clock struck the hour of midnight. Feeling chilled and nervous, he put some water on the fire to boil, so that he might have some steaming coffee before setting out. When the clock struck one, he rose, called Sam, opened the door and struck out in the direction of the Wildstrubel. He climbed for five hours continuously. He scaled the rocks with the help of his irons, and cut steps in the ice with his axe, always advancing steadily and sometimes hauling the dog after him up some steep escarpment. It was about six o'clock when he reached one of the peaks to which Gaspard often came in search of chamois. There he waited for the day to break.

The sky above became gradually paler. Then suddenly that strange radiance, which springs no one knows whence, gleamed over the great ocean of snow-clad peaks, stretching for a hundred leagues around him. The vague light seemed to arise out of the snow itself and to diffuse itself in space. One by one, the highest and farthest pinnacles were suffused by a tender rosy hue and the red sun rose from behind the great masses of the Bernese Alps. Ulrich Kunsi set forth again. Like a hunter, he went down, searching for tracks and saying to his dog:

'Seek, old man, seek.'

He was now on his way down the mountain, investigating every chasm, and sometimes sending forth a prolonged call, which quickly died away in the dumb immensity. At times he put his ear close to the ground to listen. Once he thought he heard a voice and he ran in the direction of it, shouting as he ran, but he heard nothing more, and sat down, exhausted and despairing. About mid-day he shared some food with Sam, who was as weary as himself. And again he set out on his search. When evening came, he was still walking, having accomplished fifty kilometres among the mountains. He was too far from his house to think of returning there, and too tired to drag himself along any farther. Digging a hole in the snow, he curled up in it with his dog, under cover of a blanket which he had brought with him. Man and beast lay together, each body sharing the warmth of the other, but frozen to the marrow none the less. Ulrich's mind was haunted by visions, and his limbs were shaking with cold. He could not sleep at all. When he rose, day was on the point of breaking. His legs felt as rigid as bars of iron; his resolution was so enfeebled that he almost sobbed aloud in his distress, and his heart beat so violently that he nearly collapsed with emotion whenever he fancied that he heard a sound.

The thought suddenly came to him that he too might perish of cold amidst these solitudes, and the fear of such a death whipped up his energy and roused him to fresh vigour. He was now making the descent towards the Inn, and kept falling down from weariness and picking himself up again. His dog Sam, with one paw disabled, followed far behind, limping. It was four o'clock in the afternoon before they reached the Schwarenbach. Hari was not there. Ulrich lighted a fire, had something to eat, and then fell asleep, so utterly stupefied with fatigue that he could think of nothing. He slept for a long, a very long time. It seemed as if nothing could break his repose, when suddenly he heard a voice cry 'Ulrich.' He was shaken out of his profound torpor, and started up. Was it a dream? Was it one of those strange summonses that disturb the slumber of uneasy souls? No. He could hear it still. That quivering hail had pierced his ear, had taken possession of his body, right to the tips of his nervous fingers. Beyond all doubt, there had been a cry for help, an appeal for succour. Someone had called out 'Ulrich!' Then someone must be in the vicinity of the house. There could be no question about it. He opened the door and shouted with all his strength, 'Gaspard, is that you?'

There was no reply. The silence was not broken by sound, or whisper, or groan. It was night, and the snow lay all around, ghastly in its whiteness.

The wind had risen. It was that icy wind which splits the rocks and leaves nothing alive on these forsaken altitudes. It blew in sharp, withering gusts, dealing death more surely than even the fiery blasts of the desert. Again Ulrich called out:

'Gaspard, Gaspard, Gaspard!'

He waited a little, but silence still reigned on the mountain-side, and he was forthwith stricken by a terror which shook him to the very bones. He leaped back into the inn, closed and bolted the door, and with chattering teeth collapsed into a chair. He was now sure that the appeal for help had come from his comrade, at the moment at which he was yielding up the ghost. He was as certain of that as one is of being alive or eating bread. For two days and three nights old Gaspard Hari had been wrestling with death in some hollow in one of those deep unsullied ravines, whose whiteness is more sinister than the darkness of underground caverns. For two days and three nights he had been dying, and at this very moment, while he lay in the article of death, his thoughts had turned to his comrade, and his soul, in the instant of gaining its freedom, had flown to the inn where Ulrich lay sleeping. It had exercised that mysterious and terrible power, possessed by the souls of the dead, to haunt the living. The voiceless spirit had called aloud in the overwrought soul of the sleeper, had uttered its last farewell, or, perhaps, its reproach, its curse on the man who had not searched diligently enough.

Ulrich felt its presence there, behind the walls of the house, behind the door, which he had just closed. The soul was prowling around. It was like a bird of night fluttering against a lighted window. Ulrich, distraught with terror, was ready to scream. He would have taken to flight, but dared not open the door. And never again, he felt, would he dare to open that door, for the spectre would be hovering, day and night, round the inn, until the corpse of the old guide had been recovered and laid in the consecrated earth of a cemetery.

When day broke, Ulrich regained a little confidence from the brilliance of the returning sun. He prepared his breakfast and made some soup for the dog, but after that he remained seated motionless in a chair. His heart was in agony; his thoughts turned ever to the old man, who was lying out there in the snow. When night again descended upon the mountains, new terrors assailed him. He paced to and fro in the smoke-blackened kitchen, by the dim light of a solitary candle. Up and down he strode, and always he was listening, listening, for that cry which had terrified him the night before. Might it not ring out again through the mournful silence of the outer world? He felt forlorn, poor wretch; forlorn, as never a man had been, here in this vast whiteness of snow, all alone, seven thousand feet above the inhabited world, above the dwellings of men, above the excitements, the hubbub, the noise, the thrills of life; alone in the frozen sky. He was torn by a mad desire to make his escape in whatsoever direction, by whatsoever means; to descend to Loeche, even if he had to hurl himself over the precipice. But he did not dare so much as to open the door; he felt sure that that thing outside, the dead man, would bar his passage and prevent him from leaving his comrade alone upon those heights.

As midnight approached his limbs grew weary, and fear and distress overcame him. He dreaded his bed, as one dreads a haunted spot, but yielding at last to drowsiness he sank into a chair.

Suddenly his ears were pierced by the same strident cry that he had heard the previous night. It was so shrill that Ulrich stretched out his hands to ward off the ghost, and losing his balance fell backwards on to the floor. Aroused by the noise, the dog began to howl in terror, and ran hither and thither in the room, trying to find out whence the danger threatened. When he came to the door, he sniffed at the edge of it, and began howling, snorting, and snarling, his hair bristling, his tail erect. Beside himself with terror, Kunsi rose and, grasping a stool by one leg, shouted:

'Don't come in. Don't come in. Don't come in or I'll kill you.'

Excited by his menacing tones, the dog barked furiously at the invisible enemy whom his master was challenging. Gradually Sam calmed down, and went back to lie on the hearth, but he was still uneasy; his eyes were gleaming and he was baring his fangs and growling. Ulrich, too, regained his wits; but, feeling faint with terror, he took a bottle of brandy from the sideboard and drank several glasses of it in quick succession. As his mind became duller his courage rose, and a feverish heat coursed along his veins. On the following day he ate hardly anything, confining himself to the brandy, and for some days after he lived in a state of brutish intoxication. The moment the thought of Gaspard Hari crossed his mind, he began drinking and he did not leave off until he collapsed to the ground in a drunken torpor, and lay there face downwards, snoring and helpless. Hardly had he recovered from the effects of the burning and maddening liquor, when the cry 'Ulrich!' roused him, as though a bullet had penetrated his skull. He started to his feet staggering to and fro, stretching out his hands to keep himself from falling, and calling to his dog to help him. Sam, too, appeared to be seized with his master's madness. He hurled himself against the door, scratching at it with his claws, gnawing it with his long white teeth, while Ulrich, with his head thrown back, his face turned upwards, swallowed brandy in great gulps, as though he were drinking cool water after a climb. Presently his thoughts, his memory, his terror, would be drowned in drunken oblivion.

In three weeks he had finished his entire stock of spirits.

But the only effect of his inebriation was to lull his terror to sleep. When the means for this were no longer available, his fears returned with fresh ferocity. His fixed idea, aggravated by prolonged intoxication, gained force continually in that absolute solitude, and worked its way, like a gimlet, ever deeper into his spirit. Like a wild beast in a cage, he paced his room, every now and then putting his ear to the door to listen for the voice of Gaspard's ghost, and hurling defiance at it through the wall. And when, in utter weariness, he lay down, he would again hear the voice and leap once more to his feet. At last, one night, with the courage of a coward driven to bay, he flung himself at the door and opened it, to see who it was who was calling him, and to compel him to silence. But the cold air struck him full in the face, and froze him to the marrow. He slammed the door to again, and shot the bolts, never noticing that his dog had dashed out into the open. Shivering, he threw some more wood on to the fire and sat down to warm himself. Suddenly he started. There was someone scratching at the wall and moaning.

'Go away,' he said, terror-stricken.

The answer was a melancholy wail.

His last remaining vestiges of reason were swept away by fear.

'Go away,' he cried again, and he turned hither and thither in an effort to find some corner in which he could hide himself. But the creature outside continued to wail, and passed along the front of the house, rubbing itself against the wall. Ulrich dashed to the oaken sideboard, which was full of provisions and crockery, and with superhuman strength dragged it across the room and set it against the door to act as a barricade. Then he took all the remaining furniture, mattresses, palliasses, chairs, and blockaded the window, as if in a state of siege. But the thing outside went on groaning dismally, and Ulrich himself was soon replying with groans not less lugubrious. Days and nights passed, and still these two continued to answer each other's howls.

The ghost, as it seemed to Ulrich, moved unceasingly round the house, scratching at the walls with its nails in a fierce determination to break a way through. Within the house, Ulrich crouched with his ear close to the masonry, following every movement of the thing outside, and answering all its appeals with horrifying shrieks. Then came a night when Ulrich heard no more sounds from without. Overcome with fatigue, he dropped into a chair and fell asleep immediately. When he awoke, his mind and memory were a blank. It was as if that sleep of prostration had swept his brain clean of everything. He felt hungry and took some food . . .

The winter was over. The passage of the Gemmi became practicable; and the Hauser family set forth on its journey to the inn. At the top of the first long acclivity, the two women clambered up on to their mule. They spoke about the two men, whom they expected presently to meet again. They were surprised that neither of them had descended a few days earlier, as soon as the Loeche road was practicable, to give them the news of their long winter sojourn. When they came in sight of the inn, which was still covered with a thick mantle of snow, they saw that the door and window were closed, but old Hauser was reassured by a thin column of smoke which was rising from the chimney. As he drew nearer, however, he saw on the outer threshold the skeleton of an animal. It was a large skeleton, lying on its side, and the flesh had been torn off the bones by eagles.

All three examined it.

'That must be Sam,' Madame Hauser said.

Then she called out for Gaspard, and from the inside of the house came a shrill cry like that of an animal. Old Hauser, too, shouted Gaspard's name. A second cry came from within. The father and his two sons thereupon endeavoured to open the door, but it resisted their efforts. They took a long beam out of an empty stable and used it as a battering-ram. They dashed it with all their strength against the door, which gave way with the shriek of splintering planks. The sideboard fell over on the floor with a great crash which shook the house, and revealed, standing behind it, a man whose hair came down to his shoulders, and whose beard touched his chest. His eyes were bright; his clothing was in rags.

Louise alone recognized him.

'Mamma!' she gasped, 'it is Ulrich.'

And the mother saw that it was indeed Ulrich, although his hair had turned white.

He suffered them to come near him and touch him, but

when they asked him questions he made no reply. He had to be taken down to Loeche, where the doctors certified that he was insane.

The fate of old Gaspard was never known.

During the following summer Louise Hauser came near to dying of a decline, which was attributed to the rigours of the mountain climate.

DISAPPEARANCE

Roger Malisson

The Grange was properly described as a mansion, though for some reason the estate agents had omitted this grandiose word from their brochures. At one time it had stood in its own ample park a few miles from town; now the arrival of the suburbs had placed it not far from the main road, with just a few yards of green lawn to defend it.

'Beautiful,' murmured Elizabeth Stanley when she first saw it. She had a rapport with old houses and a feeling for history. 'It's early Georgian, you know. The kids will love it.'

'You haven't seen the inside yet,' objected her husband, getting out of the car and standing beside her. He looked it over. 'I should think a flat here would be pretty pricey. You know these conversion jobs – they make you pay through the eyes and nose for a place that's all imposing address and plasterboard walls.'

Despite his reservations, the Stanleys moved in within the month. The alterations carried out to split up the house into self-contained flats had been competently done; the dividing walls were sturdy enough to keep the five families who were living there in reasonable privacy. Plenty of the original panelling was still in place on the upper floors, though the ground floor had been gutted by earlier, Victorian renovators, much to Elizabeth's disgust.

'They were barbarians,' she declared during the course of a breakfast-time lecture on the history of the house. 'They absolutely ruined the place. And did you know it isn't "The Grange" at all? Victorian pomposity! Shapton Hall was the original name.'

Her opinions were greeted with polite indifference. Neither of her two children had ever shown much interest in history, and Bill was decidedly non-academic.

'Shapton Road is the name of the road our school is on,' offered Jane, the oldest child.

'Yes, dear. Sophie, come on, you're going to be late if you dawdle like that. This whole area was once Shapton

Village – St Thomas's, near the fire station, was the parish church. Bill, do you think we should take the kids down to St Thomas's on Sunday?'

Her husband raised his eyes from the paper and shrugged. 'If you like.'

'Right, that's settled then,' she said firmly. 'We'll go to morning service and look over the church afterwards.'

It rained on Sunday and in any case they slept in, since Bill forgot to set the alarm. The flat was so cluttered and tempers so frowsty by two o'clock that Elizabeth decided, rain or no rain, they would all drive down to the church and look at it. She sorted the necessary mackintoshes and wellingtons, argued Sophie out of a tantrum, turned off the television and locked the door of the flat behind them.

The church, through the steaming May rain, was a disappointment. Squatly red brick, it had no charm whatsoever, no architectural merit, and it had clearly been built since the turn of the century. Had she not made such an issue of this expedition into local history, Elizabeth would have gladly abandoned the trip.

Inside, however, things were not so bad. The church was dry, fairly warm and quite empty. The echoing spaces, the gloom and the hanging lamps burning above the high altar took the fancy of Sophie and Jane, and they began a game of hide-and-seek among the pews.

'I think this must be the chapel of the local regiment,' said Elizabeth, peering at the tattered banners hanging near the roof. 'World War One regimental colours. What do you think, Bill?'

What her husband thought was obvious from his disgruntled expression, and Elizabeth began to think that it was a waste of time trying to impart a sense of history to the children in the face of such lethargy.

'Frankly, I'm bored,' said Bill. 'I think the skating rink would be a good idea. What do you say, kids?'

Elizabeth gave her husband a furious look, but Jane and Sophie greeted his suggestion with raptures. After that experience she made no further attempts to interest her family in the past of Shapton Village, or indeed of Shapton Hall.

Her surprise was therefore all the greater when Jane began

to fantasize about the Hall. To Elizabeth's delight she produced one day a very creditable painting of an eighteenth-century maidservant, set against the panelling in the girls' bedroom.

'Have you seen this, Bill?' She showed it to him, beaming, when the children were in bed.

'One of Jane's efforts? It's very good for an eleven-year-old.'

'Oh, of course she can't handle paint yet, but look, this costume – it's really well done. I wonder where she got the book she copied it from. All I ever see her with is Enid Blyton. Isn't it strange how you can talk to children and think they haven't taken anything in . . . and then something seeds itself in their minds – it's marvellous. I think I'll take Jane to the local history library next week.'

'Look, Liz,' said Bill, 'don't run it into the ground, will you? I mean you do tend to get carried away sometimes. Fine, you want to encourage their interest in this kind of thing, but don't forcefeed the child, okay?'

'I shall do no such thing,' replied his wife huffily. 'I'm only pleased that *one* of this family seems to be developing a worthwhile interest, and something I can share.'

In the local history library, Jane was rather bored. She seemed mainly to enjoy the microfilm readers, and gave only a passing glance to the print of Shapton Hall which hung on the wall. Once she contradicted the librarian on some point of detail that she could have known nothing of, which annoyed Elizabeth; she felt Jane was giving the impression of being a precocious, know-it-all brat.

'Why did you say that?' she asked her daughter waspishly as she took her to the coffee-bar for an afternoon treat. 'I mean about Sir Humphrey Rigby having three daughters and not two. You oughtn't to say things positively, darling, when you don't know.'

'There are three,' said Jane calmly.

'There aren't. Weren't. Look, do you remember that diagram the lady showed us, called a family tree? Well, it was a sort of map of the family who lived in our house two hundred years ago. It showed who Sir Humphrey married – he married twice, because ladies often got very ill having babies in those days.'

'His first wife died during her lying-in.'

'Exactly!' Elizabeth flushed with triumph. So Jane had been absorbing her lessons after all. Obviously she herself was not yet adept at gauging the child's learning rate. With a pang of conscience she remembered Bill's warning about forcefeeding, so she dropped the subject and applied herself to feeding Jane with cakes instead.

Jane and Sophie were Daddy's girls through and through. They seemed to have inherited all of Bill's self-possession and assertiveness, and they were very close. Sometimes Elizabeth felt a little left out of things, for recently they had begun to exclude her from their games and secrets, playing alone in their room and leaving her to the house and garden. It was a stage they had to go through, she knew, but she resented it from time to time.

The summer wore on, and the children's games of make-believe seemed to absorb them more and more strongly. Elizabeth would have discouraged them had she not once overheard Jane describing to Sophie some imaginary character in the game, obviously one of the Rigby family who had once lived in the Hall. It reminded her eerily of the little Brontë children and their fantasy world of Angria.

'Jane's really getting into history now,' she told her husband proudly one evening. 'It does surprise me. She always seemed such a placid, no-nonsense little sort. You should hear her carry on to Sophie about Lady Mary Rigby and the little Rigby girls! You can almost see them.'

'I suppose you egg her on,' said Bill, unimpressed.

'Not at all!' Elizabeth felt rebuffed. 'I never suggested the game. In fact, I haven't even let them know that I know they play it.'

'Have you noticed how peaky Sophie's been looking lately?' Bill changed the subject abruptly.

'It's the weather,' said Elizabeth. 'I think we're all feeling the heat. It'll break soon, or if it doesn't there's still the week in Scotland coming up. I think we'll keep the invitations for her birthday party down, though. I don't think a crowd of kids and a lot of noisy games are going to be much fun for any of us just now.'

The weather changed on the day of Sophie's party. A storm came in from the hills above the town and hung dry in the air for a half-hour or so before breaking, then it burst with a noise like a clap of doom. Elizabeth abandoned the game of hide-and-seek she had been organizing and rushed to console some of the wailing, smaller children.

Most of the kids there had pressed to the windows and were watching the storm with great enthusiasm, despite her demands for the curtains to be closed.

Then, when she was finally obeyed, the lights suddenly fused and left the room in a greyish darkness lit by the occasional fizzling burst of lightning visible through the thin curtains.

The effect was a little unnerving, even to Elizabeth. The room appeared to be losing its shape and becoming higher and larger. The children squealed in mock terror and ran riot.

'Sophie! Sophie! Come here at once and take Michael!' She had to scream to make herself heard above the storm and babble, and the crying child. Thrusting the little boy into Sophie's care, she shouted for Jane to fetch a torch, bitterly regretting that she had attempted this party on her own, with Bill away. It was rapidly turning into a disaster. She groped her way into the hall cupboard for the fusebox, in the dark since Jane had not appeared with a torch. Fortunately Bill always left spare fuses in a carton inside the cupboard. She fitted one, tried the light switch, and found to her annoyance that nothing was happening. Swearing uncaringly now, she changed the fuse for another, and this time the cupboard flooded with light.

Although it was only four o'clock, Elizabeth decided to let the children eat. It was the only thing she could think of to quieten them all down. She set out the food and made up the orangeade, then sat nine of them down to the party meal.

'Sophie!' She called distractedly, attempting to amuse little Michael with a paper hat. 'Tell Jane to come at once, the food's ready. Hush, Michael, there's no need to cry now – the nasty storm's all gone.'

Bill came in at the end of the meal, just as patience and the cakes were running out. His wife's rather sullen replies to his enquiries about how they had coped with the storm showed him how little fun the party had been for her. At his suggestion the children sang 'Happy Birthday' to Sophie, sorted themselves into family groups and lined up for their pieces of cake in paper napkins. Most of them had to be driven home as it was still pouring with rain, and Elizabeth gladly let him take charge.

Within twenty minutes the flat was clear, at least of children, and she began wearily straightening the wreckage. It was only when her husband came back, with Sophie chattering beside him, that she first missed Jane.

'I thought she was in the car with you. Wasn't she? Sophie, where's Jane?'

Enquiries throughout the building brought no sign of the missing child.

'Really, it's too bad,' fretted Elizabeth, 'to misbehave so badly on Sophie's birthday.'

'Jane wouldn't wander off in a storm,' said Bill tersely. 'When did you see her last?'

'She was here for the hide-and-seek, Daddy,' Sophie piped up.

Hide-and-seek. Through Elizabeth's mind flashed horrid images – the Mistletoe Bough, the door of some forgotten cellar slamming shut, children trapped in abandoned refrigerators . . . but none of that could possibly apply, surely. There were no such places in their flat.

'I bet I know where she hid!' said Sophie. 'I was going to look there first, but I didn't get the chance. Come on, I'll show you!'

Sophie led her parents to a corner of her bedroom. She pointed to the upper panel.

'In there, look.'

Elizabeth stared, bewildered, at the dark wood.

'But that's only the wall, darling . . .'

'There's a door,' said Sophie. 'I don't know where, but Jane told me all about it. She said the lady sometimes uses it for her boxes, to paint her face and stick on plasters.'

Bill was feeling the wall, running his fingers along the curved panel.

'She's right!' he cried suddenly. 'There's a crack in the wood here!'

'Which lady, Sophie?' asked Elizabeth desperately. 'Which lady showed it to Jane?'

'Lady Mary.'

Bill, paying no attention, had come back from the lounge with a brass candlestick in his hands. 'Move back.' He swung his arm and the heavy metal smashed into the wood. Something splintered inwards with a rending crash and Sophie screamed. The panel was giving, falling backwards into a cavity.

'Here, let me, let me . . .' Elizabeth thrust her hands into the hole, but was driven back by the rotten stench of foul air. With a final wrench Bill tore the strips of wood away, and the light fell in at last.

There had certainly once been a cupboard there. Dust lay thick in the tiny space.

Of Jane, however, there was no sign. Nor, in the wretched days and months that lay ahead, did any come.

It was years afterwards, when Elizabeth had long left the house and its dreadful memories, when her grief for Jane had drained to a bearable ache, and when the police no longer troubled her husband with 'identifications' that never turned out to be the right girl, but always someone else's nameless, murdered child; when Sophie was grown, and no longer remembered nightmares of dark rooms and storms, that a solution of a kind did appear.

A copy of the *Gentleman's Magazine* for 1763 came into her hands, and almost immediately the words 'History of Shapton Hall' leapt at her from the faded blue cover. Her first impulse was to put it away unread, but the next day as she took it up to throw it away, something made her turn the page and begin to read.

The article was written by one Rigby Moreton, and most of what it told she knew already. Then came the brief paragraph that numbed her mind.

> Among other notable incidents is one which has not infrequently aroused interest in those engaged in the study of scientific phenomena. Some twenty years since a child, a female, was found in the inner apartments of the Hall. Uncouthly spoken and extravagantly dressed, it was cried up by the maid who found it as a changeling, but suspected by the then master, Sir Humphrey Rigby, as a beggar's child

introduced into the Hall by thieves, with the intention that it should open the doors to them whilst the family slept. He directed accordingly that it should be questioned by the magistrates, who, however, were unable to induce it to give a rational account of itself, or its means of entry into the Hall. (These were to be more wondered at, as it was discovered in a most private place, without any of the servants having the least knowledge of its presence.) Even when it reached the years of discretion, no recollection could ever be elicited of its life prior to its appearance at the Hall, although in all other respects the child proved intelligent and possessed of a capable memory. As it was found on a night of exceptional atmospheric violence, there were not lacking those who attributed its mysterious appearance to the powers of darkness. Nevertheless, I myself have known this person for twenty years, and can declare her in every way a sober, modest and discreet woman of honest life, now married to one Alexander Prior, an apothecary's man in the parish in which she was so strangely first discovered. Her origins, however, remain, to herself no less than to the world, a perfect mystery.

Without pausing to leave a message for her family, Elizabeth drove straight to Shapton. The church still stood, as ugly as ever. The incumbent seemed quite pleased to help her with her genealogical enquiry and together they pored over the old registers until the relevant entry was found. Alexander Prior, widower and chymist, had married Jane Stanley, spinster, in the April of 1755.

'Prior . . . Let's see now,' said the Vicar, frowning. 'Yes, I know that name.' He led the way out of the church. 'This building dates from 1908, you know. It was rebuilt because the old one was unsafe. The churchyard still contains the old graves, of course.'

He led the way through the tangled, grassy paths to a gravestone half railed round, its deeply-cut inscription still legible. Elizabeth bent forward to read it.

Alexander Prior, died October 9th, 1781, aged 53. Also Jane, wife of the above, in the 72nd year of her age, 1806.

Remember, friend, as you pass by
As you are now, so once was I.
As I am now, so you shall be,
Pray for thy sins, and pray for me.

'Were they ancestors of yours?' asked the vicar, seeing her expression as she looked down at the grave.

Elizabeth stood silent for a moment.

'Jane was a relative,' she murmured finally, 'in a way.'

THE GHOST MACHINE

Roger F. Dunkley

The professor made a final check on the circuitry. Repressing an unscientific and jubilant giggle, he threw the switch. Power pulsed in a thousand sensor beams, scanning the room. The air hummed and vibrated softly like a finely tuned web.

The world's first 'ghost machine', as the press, ever facile, had labelled it, was ready.

He glanced at the screen. It glowed reassuringly but no image had materialized there. He was neither surprised nor disappointed. There had been no deaths in the room – so far as he knew: how, then, could one expect to snare and record a ghost? No, his research was only just beginning. But proof, scientific evidence of which he, nay mankind, had dreamed, was finally, he was sure, at hand. His cheeks flushed. Ultimate mysteries – he patted the control panel – would shortly be revealed. The unseen would be seen at last.

He sat, triumphantly expectant, at the console in the centre of the room. He adjusted the scanners.

A finely tuned web . . .

Abruptly there came a low knocking sound. He jumped, scattering papers, recomposed himself and opened the door.

'Puddle,' said the man. 'Jeremiah Puddle. I've come about the advertisement.'

'Ah,' said the professor. He scrutinized the newcomer and winced.

The man was small and thin and had spots. It was not a promising start. The pale face lengthened.

'You *said* you could help,' the man said despondently. He flourished a newspaper at the professor; then peered at the columns, prodding them with a reproachful forefinger. '"Do *You* Want To End It All?"' he recited. '"For Help, Contact Professor Hamnet . . ."' His sad eyes essayed a fierce glare. 'Well – I do.'

The professor hesitated, thought of his forthcoming paper, 'Death, the Last Frontier: a Psychic Breakthrough', heard the applause echoing round the Science Academies of the world, glanced at Mr Jeremiah Puddle, and closed his eyes. 'Splendid,' he said unconvincingly. 'So: you've come to take your place in the annals of History.'

Mr Puddle looked doubtful. 'I've come,' he said, 'for the suicide.' He gazed round anxiously. 'You do *do* suicides, don't you?'

The professor took his arm reassuringly. 'Under scientific compulsion. I am a mere servant,' he remarked humbly; 'it is Science herself who dictates the means which must be used to achieve her ends.'

'I see,' said the man, though he probably didn't. He glanced uneasily at his watch. 'When can we begin?' he said. 'It's my wife . . .' His meek eyes strayed apprehensively towards the door.

'She knows you're here?'

Mr Puddle shuddered. 'She'll find out. She finds out everything,' he whispered darkly. He picked nervously at a spot. The spot flared. 'That's why I've come to you,' he said, and launched forthwith into a despairing catalogue of marital misadventures.

Mrs Puddle, it transpired, was loud and somewhat encumbered with large limbs. She talked incessantly. She had, it seemed, talked her way steadily through their marriage, pausing only at statutory intervals to eat and sleep. Her words were as numerous as her themes were limited. She talked about Jeremiah's faults, his failures and his passivity.

'She's right,' he concluded. 'I'm a failure. I need help. I tried the weedkiller, but it went wrong.'

The professor raised an eyebrow and readjusted his face to blend a hint of curiosity with the patient sympathy.

'Home-made wine,' said the man called Puddle. 'Parsnip. I drank from the wrong container.' The ghost of a smile scuttered across his sallow features and was gone. 'I was nearly happy then,' he reminisced. 'Just the once.'

He sank into silence. Pathos hovered about him. The machine murmured, probed the still spaces of the room, and waited. The professor seized the silence.

'Yes,' he said. 'Well,' he added. He attempted to rub his hands briskly, but he knew he was wringing them – now that the moment had come to assist his first subject. 'So . . . Down to business, eh?' He unlocked and pulled open a drawer. 'How – ah – would you like it? . . . Your death,' he prompted.

Something approaching life stirred in Mr Puddle's eyes. He watched the professor draw forth a length of rope. The eyes dulled. He shook his head.

'Tried it,' he said. 'The noose came undone. I slipped off the chair and sprained my wrist.' The memory welled up unhappily. 'It *hurt. And* she made me go without dinner for two days.'

The spots throbbed pink with indignation.

'It was the same when I jumped out of the bedroom window.'

The professor tried to turn his yawn into a cough; he succeeded in a hiccup. 'What happened?' he asked brightly.

'I fell on top of her,' said Jeremiah Puddle. The old ignominy shook his unambitious frame. 'She caught me. In her arms. And carried me back into the house.'

The professor reached into the drawer. 'Gun?'

'No bullets. She locked them away.'

'Bullets!' The professor loaded the gun and waved it at him encouragingly.

'Too loud,' said Mr Puddle. 'I was deaf for a week after I first tried it.' He shuffled miserably. 'And I shot the budgie,' he added, 'by mistake.'

The professor's hand twitched temptingly on the trigger. 'Too untidy,' he thought and laid the revolver on the desk. He dismissed the razor blade for the same reason. His hand hesitated over the hypodermic and came to rest on the tablets. He held the phial aloft. The purple pills gave a low rattle. Speedy, silent, painless and tidy, he thought.

Enthusiasm flirted with doubt on Mr Puddle's yellow face. 'I'm not very good at swallowing tablets,' he said. 'I bought five hundred aspirin once . . .'

Professor Hamnet hastily curtailed the reminiscence. 'One capsule will do the trick,' he said. He filled a glass with water and offered it temptingly. 'Perhaps you'd like to lie down.' He ushered the man towards the couch strategically placed for maximum exposure to the detector field.

The centre of the web.

'Make yourself comfortable,' he said, his voice as soothing and concerned as an over-fastidious nanny's. 'Rest,' he said.

'In peace,' said Mr Puddle. 'That was a sort of joke,' he explained. 'I don't often make jokes.'

Submissively he received the glass in one hand, the pill in the other.

'Is this – it?' he asked.

The professor's pulse changed into higher gear. This was it, indeed. The spirit of Jeremiah Puddle was poised for flight; his psychic detectors were trained on the corporeal Puddle awaiting the release. It was an auspicious moment. The professor paused. A speech, he felt, was appropriate to so historical an event. He cleared his throat. Words, however, eluded him.

'We are gathered here . . .' he began. 'Today . . .'

'Excuse me.' The watery eyes turned hopefully upwards. 'Do I swallow it now?'

The professor shook his head. 'Today,' he repeated, 'you embark on a momentous voyage, a voyage of discovery into that "undiscovered country", as Shakespeare so movingly described it, "from whose – thingy – no traveller returns . . ."'

'"No traveller returns,"' echoed the man. He closed his eyes and an alien look of peace and ecstasy settled over his pimpled features.

The professor stretched out his arm; it seemed the right thing to do. His voice was tremulous with excitement and a touch of indigestion. 'Go forth, Jeremiah Puddle,' he pronounced. 'Go forth into Death and History!'

The man raised his glass. Eternity waited.

'Hold on a sec.' Professor Hamnet caught his arm. 'Don't go yet. Your suicide note. Sign here. Thanks. Indemnity,' he murmured. 'The law. Right. As you were. Bully off. Cheers.'

Mr Puddle placed the tablet carefully in his mouth, raised his glass and gulped.

He gulped again.

A seraphic contentment suffused his face. The Puddle pimples seemed to fade and assume an otherworldly hue.

The professor watched the screen with eager concentration.

Downstairs an angry door banged; the building trembled.

The white glow of the screen remained obstinately unblemished. The professor re-tuned the scanners. He turned the gain control to maximum. The circuits hummed industriously.

He peered more closely, attempting to pierce beyond the veil.

But nothing registered on the screen.

The veil refused to part.

Then light cleft his brain. The professor rose abruptly, choking back an exultant laugh. He saw it all: *there was nothing to see! That* was the point. Puddle had gone. Death was final. No traveller returned because nothing survived. Oblivion not Survival: that was The Answer.

He paced the room in pursuit of ultimate truths, completing several circuits of the recumbent Puddle. His mind raced on.

Eliminate the spirit, the soul. What, then, was a ghost, doomed endlessly to walk the same walks, groan the same groans, rattle the same chains? What else, he assured himself, but a psychic recording, a dead memory vibrating eternally in the ether. But where then, he demanded of himself, was the recording of the deceased Puddle? The screen was conspicuously empty. Puddle had escaped without registering a trace of *his* passing.

He glanced at the face on the couch, glowing with serenity. There lay his answer! *Jeremiah Puddle was happy. Too happy.* Whoever heard of a placid, contented ghost? The professor found himself standing excitedly on tip-toe. The man – the truth had to be told – had been a failure even in his dying. He had been completely devoid of the passion, the energy, the misery needed to blaze the waves of his dying moments on to the surrounding air and become a successful ghost – the first ghost in Professor Hamnet's machine.

Startled, and then annoyed, the professor heard a second door slam at the end of the corridor.

He looked down reproachfully at Puddle and shook his head. Evidence. The world required proof, pictures.

What he really needed, he realized, was a research assistant who could be relied upon to die a lively, passionate, violent sort of death . . .

'What! . . .'

The door had crashed open and hung crookedly on its splintered hinges.

The figure was large and awesome. She seemed about to roar. Her glittering eyes lit on the body on the couch and she strode across to it. The room trembled. The roar escaped.

'What have you done with my man?'

The professor retreated. Mrs Puddle advanced. He opened his mouth but only an emaciated squeak got out. He lunged forward and seized the revolver.

'Aha,' he said. He waved it, suddenly triumphant. A violent death! It was self-defence. And it meant a place in the annals of history.

But Mrs Puddle was an ardent admirer of Hollywood movies of the more criminal kind. Her ungainly limbs moved with improbable but lethal dexterity. The professor staggered to his feet in the corner and found himself staring at Mrs Puddle's arm. At the end of the arm was the single, black eye of his revolver.

'My poor little husband,' she said. 'You killed him.'

Panic surged through the professor. His nerves screamed and he gave vent to a resounding hiccup.

'My research! . . .' he blurted.

'Murderer!' she said and pulled the trigger.

Eyes dilated, arms flung upwards, the professor, protesting, made his earthly exit. He was right. It was an untidy way to die.

Mrs Puddle turned, seized her late husband and flung him over her shoulder. She thumped his back vigorously.

He coughed.

'There, there,' she said.

Then he choked.

Then a purple capsule hit the floor with a clatter.

Jeremiah Puddle's eyes opened sadly on the world once more. He beheld his wife. His face sagged. She put him down, embraced him, straightened his tie, and took his hand.

She noticed the screen for the first time and stared at him disdainfully. 'What a time to be watching television!' she said. She cast only a cursory glance at the sequence of images which now haunted the glowing screen: the cornered man cowering with upraised arms, his mouth opened wide in indignant terror – an eternal psychic action replay.

'And a gangster film at that!' She tugged his arm. 'Time to go home,' she said. 'Success. We won. You're safe now.'

Jeremiah Puddle's spots flushed crimson.

'Yes, dear,' he said. 'Success . . .'

The machine purred.

THE ROCKER

Oliver Onions

There was little need for the swart gipsies to explain, as they stood knee-deep in the snow round the bailiff of the Abbey Farm, what it was that had sent them. The unbroken whiteness of the uplands told that, and, even as they spoke, there came up the hill the dark figures of the farm men with shovels, on their way to dig out the sheep. In the summer, the bailiff would have been the first to call the gipsies vagabonds and roost-robbers; now . . . they had women with them too.

'The hares and foxes were down four days ago, and the liquid-manure pump's like a snowman,' the bailiff said . . . 'Yes, you can lie in the laithes and welcome – if you can find 'em. Maybe you'll help us find our sheep too – '

The gipsies had done so. Coming back again, they had had some ado to discover the spot where their three caravans made a hummock of white against a broken wall.

The women – they had four women with them – began that afternoon to weave the mats and baskets they hawked from door to door; and in the forenoon of the following day one of them, the black-haired, soft-voiced quean whom the bailiff had heard called Annabel, set her babe in the sling on her back, tucked a bundle of long cane-loops under her oxter, and trudged down between eight-foot walls of snow to the Abbey Farm. She stood in the latticed porch, dark and handsome against the whiteness, and then, advancing, put her head into the great hall-kitchen.

'Has the lady any chairs for the gipsy woman to mend?' she asked in a soft and insinuating voice . . .

They brought her the old chairs; she seated herself on a box in the porch; and there she wove the strips of cane in and out, securing each one with a little wooden peg and a tap of her hammer. The child remained in the sling at her back, taking the breast from time to time over her shoulder; and the silver wedding ring could be seen as she whipped the cane back and forth.

As she worked, she cast curious glances into the old hall-kitchen. The snow outside cast a pallid, upward light on the heavy ceiling-beams; this was reflected in the polished stone floor; and the children, who at first had shyly stopped their play, seeing the strange woman in the porch – the nearest thing they had seen to gipsies before had been the old itinerant glazier with his frame of glass on his back – resumed it, but still eyed her from time to time. In the ancient walnut chair by the hearth sat the old, old lady who had told them to bring the chairs. Her hair, almost as white as the snow itself, was piled up on her head *à la Marquise*; she was knitting; but now and then she allowed the needle in the little wooden sheath at her waist to lie idle, closed her eyes, and rocked softly in the old walnut chair.

'Ask the woman who is mending the chairs whether she is warm enough there,' the old lady said to one of the children; and the child went to the porch with the message.

'Thank you, little missie – thank you, lady dear – Annabel is quite warm,' said the soft voice; and the child returned to the play.

It was a childish game of funerals at which the children played. The hand of Death, hovering over the dolls, had singled out Flora, the articulations of whose sawdust body were seams and whose boots were painted on her calves of fibrous plaster. For the greater solemnity, the children had made themselves sweeping trains of the garments of their elders, and those with cropped curls had draped their heads with shawls, the fringes of which they had combed out with their fingers to simulate hair – long hair, such as Sabrina, the eldest, had hanging so low down her back that she could almost sit on it. A cylindrical-bodied horse, convertible (when his flat head came out of its socket) into a locomotive, headed the sad *cortège*; then came the defunct Flora; then came Jack, the raffish sailor doll, with other dolls; and the children followed with hushed whisperings.

The youngest of the children passed the high-backed walnut chair in which the old lady sat. She stopped.

'Aunt Rachel – ' she whispered, slowly and gravely opening very wide and closing very tight her eyes.

'Yes, dear?'

'Flora's dead!'

The old lady, when she smiled, did so less with her lips

than with her faded cheeks. So sweet was her face that you could not help wondering, when you looked on it, how many men had also looked upon it and loved it. Somehow, you never wondered how many of them had been loved in return.

'I'm so sorry, dear,' Aunt Rachel, who in reality was a great-aunt, said. 'What did she die of this time?'

'She died of . . . Brown Titus . . . 'n now she's going to be buried in a grave as little as her bed.'

'In a what, dear?'

'As little . . . dread . . . as little as my bed . . . you say it, Sabrina.'

'She means, Aunt Rachel,

"Teach me to live that I may dread
The Grave as little as my bed."'

Sabrina, the eldest, interpreted.

'Ah! . . . But won't you play at cheerful things, dears?'

'Yes, we will, presently, Aunt Rachel; gee up, horse! . . . Shall we go and ask the chair-woman if she's warm enough?'

'Do, dears.'

Again the message was taken, and this time it seemed as if Annabel, the gipsy, was not warm enough, for she gathered up her loops of cane and brought the chair she was mending a little way into the hall-kitchen itself. She sat down on the square box they used to cover the sewing machine.

'Thank you, lady dear,' she murmured, lifting her handsome almond eyes to Aunt Rachel. Aunt Rachel did not see the long, furtive, curious glance. Her own eyes were closed, as if she was tired; her cheeks were smiling; one of them had dropped a little to one shoulder, as it might have dropped had she held in her arms a babe; and she was rocking, softly, slowly, the rocker of the chair making a little regular noise on the polished floor.

The gipsy woman beckoned to one of the children.

'Tell the lady, when she wakes, that I will tack a strip of felt to the rocker, and then it will make no noise at all,' said the low and wheedling voice; and the child retired again.

The interment of Flora proceeded . . .

An hour later Flora had taken up the burden of Life again. It was as Angela, the youngest, was chastising her for some offence that Sabrina, the eldest, looked with wondering eyes on the babe in the gipsy's sling. She approached on tiptoe.

'May I look at it, please?' she asked timidly.

The gipsy set one shoulder forward, and Sabrina put the shawl gently aside, peering at the dusky brown morsel within.

'Some time, perhaps – if I'm very careful – ' Sabrina ventured diffidently – 'if I'm *very* careful – may I hold it?'

Before replying, the gipsy once more turned her almond eyes towards Aunt Rachel's chair. Aunt Rachel had been awakened for the conclusion of Flora's funeral, but her eyes were closed again now, and once more her cheek was dropped in that tender suggestive little gesture, and she rocked. But you could see that she was not properly asleep . . . It was, somehow, less to Sabrina, still peering at the babe in the sling, than to Aunt Rachel, apparently asleep, that the gipsy seemed to reply.

'You'll know some day, little missis, that a wean knows its own pair of arms,' her seductive voice came.

And Aunt Rachel heard. She opened her eyes with a start. The little regular noise of the rocker ceased. She turned her head quickly; tremulously she began to knit again; and, as her eyes rested on the sidelong eyes of the gipsy woman, there was an expression in them that almost resembled fright.

They began to deck the great hall-kitchen for Christmas, but the snow still lay thick over hill and valley, and the gipsies' caravans remained by the broken wall where the drifts had overtaken them. Though all the chairs were mended, Annabel still came daily to the farm, sat on the box they used to cover the sewing machine, and wove mats. As she wove them, Aunt Rachel knitted, and from time to time fragments of talk passed between the two women. It was always the white-haired lady who spoke first, and Annabel made all sorts of salutes and obeisances with her eyes before replying.

'I have not seen your husband,' Aunt Rachel said to Annabel one day. (The children at the other end of the apartment had converted a chest into an altar, and were solemnizing the nuptials of the resurrected Flora and Jack, the raffish sailor-doll.)

Annabel made roving play with her eyes. 'He is up at the caravans, lady dear,' she replied. 'Is there anything Annabel can bid him do?'

'Nothing, thank you,' said Aunt Rachel.

For a minute the gipsy watched Aunt Rachel, and then she got up from the sewing-machine box and crossed the floor. She leaned so close towards her that she had to put up a hand to steady the babe at her back.

'Lady dear,' she murmured with irresistible softness, 'your husband died, didn't he?'

On Aunt Rachel's finger was a ring, but it was not a wedding ring. It was a hoop of pearls.

'I have never had a husband,' she said.

The gipsy glanced at the ring. 'Then that is – ?'

'That is a betrothal ring,' Aunt Rachel replied.

'Ah! . . .' said Annabel.

Then, after a minute, she drew still closer. Her eyes were fixed on Aunt Rachel's, and the insinuating voice was very low.

'Ah! . . . And did *it* die too, lady dear?'

Again came that quick, half-affrighted look into Aunt Rachel's face. Her eyes avoided those of the gipsy, sought them, and avoided them again.

'Did what die?' she asked slowly and guardedly . . .

The child at the gipsy's back did not need suck; nevertheless, Annabel's fingers worked at her bosom, and she moved the sling. As the child settled, Annabel gave Aunt Rachel a long look.

'Why do you rock?' she asked slowly.

Aunt Rachel was trembling. She did not reply. In a voice soft as sliding water the gipsy continued:

'Lady dear, we are a strange folk to you, and even among us there are those who shuffle the pack of cards and read the palm when silver has been put upon it, knowing nothing . . . But some of us *see* – some of us *see*.'

It was more than a minute before Aunt Rachel spoke.

'You are a woman, and you have your babe at your breast now . . . Every woman sees the thing you speak of.'

But the gipsy shook her head. 'You speak of seeing with the heart. I speak of eyes – these eyes.'

Again came a long pause. Aunt Rachel had given a little start, but had become quiet again. When at last she spoke it was in a voice scarcely audible.

'That cannot be. I know what you mean, but it cannot be . . . He died on the eve of his wedding. For my bridal clothes they made me black garments instead. It is long ago, and now I wear neither black nor white, but – ' her hands made a gesture. Aunt Rachel always dressed as if to suit a sorrow that Time had deprived of bitterness, in such a tender and fleecy grey as one sees in the mists that lie like lawn over hedgerow and copse early of a midsummer's morning. 'Therefore,' she resumed, 'your heart may see, but your eyes cannot see that which never was.'

But there came a sudden note of masterfulness into the gipsy's voice.

'With my eyes – *these* eyes,' she repeated, pointing to them.

Aunt Rachel kept her own eyes obstinately on her knitting needles. 'None except I have seen it. It is not to be seen,' she said.

The gipsy sat suddenly erect.

'It is not so. Keep still in your chair,' she ordered, 'and I will tell you when – '

It was a curious thing that followed. As if all the will went out of her, Aunt Rachel sat very still; and presently her hands fluttered and dropped. The gipsy sat with her own hands folded over the mat on her knees. Several minutes passed; then, slowly, once more that sweetest of smiles stole over Aunt Rachel's cheeks. Once more her head dropped. Her hands moved. Noiselessly on the rockers that the gipsy had padded with felt the chair began to rock. Annabel lifted one hand.

'*Dovo se li*,' she said. 'It is there.'

Aunt Rachel did not appear to hear her. With that ineffable smile still on her face, she rocked . . .

Then, after some minutes, there crossed her face such a look as visits the face of one who, waking from sleep, strains his faculties to recapture some blissful and vanishing vision . . .

'*Jal* – it is gone,' said the gipsy woman.

Aunt Rachel opened her eyes again. She repeated dully after Annabel:

'It is gone.'

'Ghosts,' the gipsy whispered presently, 'are of the dead. Therefore it must have lived.'

But again Aunt Rachel shook her head. 'It never lived.'

'You were young, and beautiful? . . .'

Still the shake of the head. 'He died on the eve of his wedding. They took my white garments away and gave me black ones. How then could it have lived?'

'Without the kiss, no . . . But sometimes a woman will lie through her life, and at the graveside still will lie . . . Tell me the truth.'

But they were the same words that Aunt Rachel repeated: 'He died on the eve of his wedding; they took away my wedding garments . . .' From her lips a lie could hardly issue. The gipsy's face became grave . . .

She broke another long silence.

'I believe,' she said at last. 'It is a new kind – but no more wonderful than the other. The other I have seen, now I have seen this also. Tell me, does it come to any other chair?'

'It was his chair; he died in it,' said Aunt Rachel.

'And you – shall you die in it?'

'As God wills.'

'Has . . . *other life* . . . visited it long?'

'Many years; but it is always small; it never grows.'

'To their mothers babes never grow. They remain ever babes . . . None other has ever seen it?'

'Except yourself, none. I sit here; presently it creeps into my arms; it is small and warm; I rock, and then . . . it goes.'

'Would it come to another chair?'

'I cannot tell. I think not. It was his chair.'

Annabel mused. At the other end of the room Flora was now bestowed on Jack, the disreputable sailor. The gipsy's eyes rested on the bridal party . . .

'Yet another might see it – '

'None has.'

'No; but yet . . . The door does not always shut behind us suddenly. Perhaps one who has toddled but a step or two over the threshold might, by looking back, catch a glimpse . . . What is the name of the smallest one?'

'Angela.'

'That means "angel" . . . Look, the doll who died yesterday is now being married . . . It may be that Life has not yet sealed the little one's eyes. Will you let Annabel ask her if she sees what it is you hold in your arms?'

Again the voice was soft and wheedling . . .

'No, Annabel,' said Aunt Rachel faintly.

'Will you rock again?'

Aunt Rachel made no reply.

'Rock . . .' urged the cajoling voice.

But Aunt Rachel only turned the betrothal ring on her finger. Over at the altar Jack was leering at his new-made bride, past decency; and little Angela held the wooden horse's head, which had parted from its body.

'Rock, and comfort yourself – ' tempted the voice.

Then slowly Aunt Rachel rose from her chair.

'No, Annabel,' she said gently. 'You should not have spoken. When the snow melts you will go, and come no more; why then did you speak? It was mine. It was not meant to be seen by another. I no longer want it. Please go.'

The swarthy woman turned her almond eyes on her once more.

'You cannot live without it,' she said as she also rose . . .

And as Jack and his bride left the church on the reheaded horse, Aunt Rachel walked with hanging head from the apartment.

Thenceforward, as day followed day, Aunt Rachel rocked no more; and with the packing and partial melting of the snow the gipsies up at the caravans judged it time to be off about their business. It was on the morning of Christmas Eve that they came down in a body to the Abbey Farm to express their thanks to those who had befriended them; but the bailiff was not there. He and the farm men had ceased work, and were down at the church, practising the carols. Only Aunt Rachel sat, still and knitting, in the black walnut chair; and the children played on the floor.

A night in the toy-box had apparently bred discontent between Jack and Flora – or perhaps they sought to keep their countenances before the world; at any rate, they sat on opposite sides of the room, Jack keeping boon company with the lead soldiers, his spouse reposing, her lead-balanced eyes closed, in the broken clockwork motor-car. With the air of performing some vaguely momentous ritual, the children were kissing one another beneath the bunch of mistletoe that hung from the centre beam. In the intervals of kissing they told one another in whispers that Aunt Rachel was not very well, and Angela woke Flora to tell her that Aunt Rachel had Brown Titus also.

'Stay you here; I will give the lady dear our thanks,' said Annabel to the group of gipsies gathered about the porch; and she entered the great hall-kitchen. She approached the chair in which Aunt Rachel sat.

There was obeisance in the bend of her body, but command in her long almond eyes, as she spoke.

'Lady dear, you must rock or you cannot live.'

Aunt Rachel did not look up from her work.

'Rocking, I should not live long,' she replied.

'We are leaving you.'

'All leave me.'

'Annabel fears she has taken away your comfort.'

'Only for a little while. The door closes behind us, but it opens again.'

'But for that little time, rock – '

Aunt Rachel shook her head.

'No. It is finished. Another has seen . . . Say goodbye to your companions; they are very welcome to what they have had; and God speed you.'

'They thank you, lady dear . . . Will you not forget what Annabel saw, and rock?'

'No more.'

Annabel stooped and kissed the hand that bore the betrothal hoop of pearls. The other hand Aunt Rachel placed for a moment upon the smoky head of the babe in the sling. It trembled as it rested there, but the tremor passed, and Annabel, turning once at the porch, gave her a last look. Then she departed with her companions.

That afternoon, Jack and Flora had shaken down to wedlock as married folk should, and sat together before the board spread with the dolls' tea-things. The pallid light in the great hall-kitchen faded; the candles were lighted; and then the children, first borrowing the stockings of their elders to hang at the bed's foot, were packed off early – for it was the custom to bring them down again at midnight for the carols. Aunt Rachel had their good-night kisses, not as she had them every night, but with the special ceremony of the mistletoe.

Other folk, grown folk, sat with Aunt Rachel that evening; but the old walnut chair did not move upon its rockers. There was merry talk, but Aunt Rachel took no part in it. The board was spread with ale and cheese and spiced loaf for the carol-singers; and the time drew near for their coming.

When at midnight, faintly on the air from the church below, there came the chiming of Christmas morning, all bestirred themselves.

'They'll be here in a few minutes,' they said. 'Somebody go and bring the children down'; and within a very little while subdued noises were heard outside, and the lifting of the latch of the yard gate. The children were in their night-gowns, hardly fully awake; a low voice outside was heard giving orders; and then there arose on the night the carol.

'Hush!' they said to the wondering children; 'listen! . . .'

It was the Cherry Tree Carol that rose outside, of how sweet Mary, the Queen of Galilee, besought Joseph to pluck the cherries for her Babe, and Joseph refused; and the voices of the singers, that had begun hesitatingly, grew strong and loud and free.

'. . . and Joseph wouldn't pluck the cherries,' somebody was whispering to the tiny Angela . . .

'Mary said to Cherry Tree,
"Bow down to my knee,
That I may pluck cherries
For my Babe and me."'

the carollers sang; and 'Now listen, darling,' the one who held Angela murmured . . .

'The uppermost spray then
Bowed down to her knee;
"Thus you may see, Joseph,
These cherries are for me."

"O, eat your cherries, Mary,
Give them your Babe now;
O, eat your cherries, Mary,
That grew upon the bough."'

The little Angela, within the arms that held her, murmured, 'It's the gipsies, isn't it, Mother?'

'No, darling. The gipsies have gone. It's the carol-singers, singing because Jesus was born.'

'But, Mother . . . it *is* the gipsies, isn't it? . . . 'Cos look . . .'

'Look where?'

'At Aunt Rachel, Mother . . . The gipsy woman wouldn't go without her little baby, would she?'

'No, she wouldn't do that.'

'Then has she *lent* it to Aunt Rachel, like I lend my new toys sometimes?'

The mother glanced across at Aunt Rachel, and then gathered the night-gowned figure more closely.

'The darling's only half awake,' she murmured . . . 'Poor Aunt Rachel's sleepy too . . .'

Aunt Rachel, her head dropped, her hands lightly folded as if about some shape that none saw but herself, her face again ineffable with that sweet and peaceful smile, was once more rocking softly in her chair.

THE CAPE COD POLTERGEIST

Margaret Chilvers Cooper

'You had to watch out for Sam,' Mr Tuttle said. 'He always had the last word.' As if held back by a stubborn hand, the door of the Cohoon house appeared to have a mind of its own, but gave suddenly and he skidded across the living-room floor beyond the rug's reach, maintaining his balance by flailing his arms like stabilizing wings. Mr Tuttle was the loan officer of the Cape Reveres Bank, which held the mortgage on the house my husband and I were building on Buzzards Bay, and we had turned to him for help in finding a place to stay until we could move in. Mr Tuttle had taken us to the Cohoon house immediately.

'My cousin and I are heirs. I can't clear the stuff out until she gets here.' With a glance around the room, he raised bushy eyebrows, a counterbalance to a balding head.

'If it were left to me,' he continued, 'I'd call in a dealer and –' he opened wide his fingers – 'out.'

Built into a stand of cedars and pines, the cottage was almost invisible from the dirt road, but the immediate area in the back had been cleared to give a view of a pond where Canada geese had taken temporary refuge. The living quarters appeared to be all on one floor, but when we went down to the cellar, we found a storage area with a washing machine which looked new enough to have a gift ribbon wrapped around it, and extending the rest of the length of the house, a panelled room furnished with a braid rug, a Franklin stove, a partner to an old Hitchcock rocker, and a smoking-stand with a tray stuffed with stale cigar butts, the odour of which rested in the room since the small half windows were all nailed shut. There was also a rudimentary lavatory, an apparent refuge for Sam, for an antique shaving-cup with S. Cohoon in gold letters on it was on the top of the toilet, and in the cupboard above the sink was a man's comb, a razor, and a cake of Lifebuoy soap. Beside the cup was a bottle marked Listerine, which had a curious, dark colour.

With an eye on his effects, I remembered Mr Tuttle's remark

and asked, 'You had to watch out for Sam?'

'Oh, yes.' Mr Tuttle smiled. 'Myra, his wife, was always nagging him to help with something around the house. Sam wasn't much on work. When he got tired of it, he threw things.' Picking up an imaginary object, he raised his right arm like a pitcher and sailed out his ball over the plate. An expression of male satisfaction slipped across his face and floated by me to my husband. 'You women make too much of these niggling chores.'

Recalling a glimpse of several good pieces of amethyst and Early Lace glass on the what-not in the living-room, I pitched one of my own. 'I notice he missed the art glass upstairs.'

But Mr Tuttle was a lawyer, as well as a loan officer, and able to switch to a defensive ground. 'Sam didn't smash anything of real value. He had the Yankee thrift.' He chuckled. 'He just kept Myra worried that he would.'

Again that look floated by, but this time it missed Jay completely. He had opened Sam's bottle of Listerine and was sniffing. 'Brandy,' he commented. He put a little on his finger and sipped. 'Good brand.'

Mr Tuttle said, 'Sam never spared himself in that way.'

As we went back up the stairs, I had the feeling that there were three male chauvinists against one unliberated female: Mr Tuttle, my husband, and Sam Cohoon. However, once Sam's house became our lodgings, I tried to push the feeling away. If in the night I thought that I heard footsteps pacing the cellar, or the creak of a rocker protesting its swaying, and on more than one occasion caught the whiff of a strong cigar, I said nothing, as little by little we shed our city carapace. Twice Mr Tuttle called to invite Jay to play golf in Provincetown on a Saturday, but he put him off. Meals in the old-fashioned kitchen were lazy. We swam and fished for trout in the pond and, like the geese, drifted along as if on a second honeymoon, until one day, the geese flew off, our idyllic boat grounded, and I climbed to shore.

'Look,' I said, 'this place has got to be cleaned. It is filthy.'

My husband put on his tolerant-of-women's-foibles expression. 'Don't you think you are inclined to exaggerate? Filthy sounds as if it is X-rated.'

'Maybe. But Sam Cohoon did not throw the things that are here.' I emphasized the *are*. I added, 'Mr Tuttle said that

Sam outlived Myra by several weeks. It's easy to see that he survived the energy crisis by saving on work.'

Jay said, 'We've been sticking around here too much. Why don't we take the day off and go down the Cape?'

He was looking at me with a seductive blue eye, but I happened to meet the dark eyes of a picture hanging on the wall which Mr Tuttle had said was Myra Cohoon and thought her expression dour. I said to it, 'We've simply got to clean.'

With a shrug, Jay put down his pipe. 'It's Saturday. If you won't go, I may as well call Tuttle. He's been after me to shoot a few at that West to the Sun course in Provincetown.'

'But,' I protested, 'I thought that you would help me.'

'Ho, I'd only be a nuisance,' he assured me. 'I don't know one end of the vacuum-cleaner from the other.' On his way to the phone he paused with the air of a man who has found a sensible solution to female peccadilloes. 'The time to do cleaning is in the winter when the weather is bad.' He raised encouraging eyebrows, but I shook my head and he made the date for Mr Tuttle to pick him up.

While the expression filthy in regard to the condition of the house may have been a trifle exaggerated, there was plenty of work to be done. I was embarrassed to face Myra's reproachful gaze which I thought brightened when I walked by with a basket full of clothes for the laundry. For it to be so new, she must have battled for that washing machine for years. With a flip of the wrist, I set it in motion. While it ran with that pleasant sound of work done without effort, I swept up the floor, dusted the rocker, threw the cigar butts in the trash, washed the shaving cup with Sam's name on it, and took the bottle of Listerine with its singular contents upstairs, where I poured a little into a bowl to mix with the other ingredients that go to make a nut loaf, a favourite of my husband's, who was now exposed to Mr Tuttle's denigrating remarks on women's work. While the cake baked, I had a go with the vacuum across the hooked rug in the living-room. When the power shut off, and the whirring noise in the cellar of the washer ceased, I was about half-way across. I searched the cellar for a fuse, but there was nothing except a bunch of nails in Sam's tool chest and an old Savage revolver. When I remembered the cake, it stared at me sullenly from the cold oven, a thick mess of paste-like stuff used for wallpapering.

Thankful that Jay had left me the car, I set out to buy a fuse, but when I opened the garage door I found in the left, flat, front tyre a long nail like those I had seen in Sam's tool chest. Returning to the house, I tried the lights – all out – and discovered that the refrigerator was defrosting. I put in a call for an electrician, piled as much of the contents of the refrigerator into a sandwich as I possibly could, took my lunch and ate it beside the pond, where I fell asleep. When I awoke, the phone was ringing.

'I don't know when I'll get home,' my husband said. 'Tuttle rammed his car into a parked station-wagon.'

'Are you all right?' I exclaimed.

'Of course,' he answered. 'It's the car. They have to replace the radiator. They're trying to find one.' He lowered his voice. 'He's a rotten driver.'

'How was his golf?' I asked.

'The same. Takes ten minutes for every putt, and cheats on his score. We'll be here all night!'

'All night!' I woke up to my situation. 'Jay,' I cried, 'come home without him. Hire a car! Take a plane! Don't leave me alone with . . .'

'What?' he asked. 'I can't hear you. I am in one of those glassed-in jobs by the road and the traffic's starting to roll. See you later.' He hung up.

When I passed Myra's photograph, I thought she looked worried, but what could she do? She was only a picture, but I was alone in the house with a malicious spirit which I was beginning to believe was Sam Cohoon. I tried the electrician one more time, but got no answer. I was still not convinced that I was going to be left alone in the dark, but after I had dined on tomatoes, cheddar and cold macaroni, I knew that I was, and went down to the cellar and brought up the revolver and a pile of Sam's sports magazines, the only reading matter there was in the house. I then removed Myra's pewter candlesticks off the mantel over the fireplace and put one in the bedroom where I read *Hunt and Fish Magazine* until my eyes started to close. Before I went to sleep I placed a kitchen chair over the back door knob and reversed a hanging pot of ivy from the window next to the front door so that it hung from its metal arm across the door. But, in spite of these precautions, I believed that trouble was inside the house. I awoke to a series of thuds, rapid cracks, and sounds like steps running back and forth beneath me. I huddled under the covers. If it were a burglar, what did I care? Then I remembered that, in spite of my precautions with the back door and the front, the cellar door was open. Grabbing the revolver in one hand and the candle in the other, I ran through the house to the kitchen and peered into the black abyss below.

'Stop!' I commanded, 'or I'll shoot!'

Like an angry drum, the banging continued.

'Stop!' I screamed. 'I mean it, I will shoot.'

Thumping and cracking, the defiant noise accelerated into an angry crescendo. Taking aim, I fired into the cellar. There was silence. I listened, but nothing moved. With trembling knees, I sank into a kitchen chair, and held the gun pointing into the dark hole of the stairs and waited. Even a summer night can bring a chill. My teeth chattered to the tune of the cicadas as my candle burned close to the stick. It was almost gone when Jay unlocked the back door and knocked over the chair.

'I've just killed someone,' I said.

He tried the light switch, which gave a heartless click, took in the situation, picked up the faltering candle, and went down into the cellar.

He called up to me, 'Hit the lally column and ricocheted into Sam's rocker. Bull's eye!' He came back up. 'Say,' he said, 'you could get to be a trick shot with a little practice. You must have had a nightmare.'

'It wasn't a nightmare. There was someone down there making a terrible noise.'

'I better unload this.' He picked up the pistol and the thing went off.

'There,' I exclaimed. 'You see? I've been alone with him all day.' Glancing down at the bullet buried in the kitchen floor six inches from his right big toe, he said, 'You left the safety catch off. Alone with whom?'

'Sam Cohoon,' I said.

'No one could get in down there; the windows are all nailed shut.' Putting an arm around me, he led me to the bedroom. 'You were dreaming.'

'But,' I protested, 'you don't know what happened: the laundry stopped, the cake was ruined, the fridge is defrosting, he stuck a nail in the front left tyre.'

'Sam should have put in a 220-volt line for that washing machine. Remind me to tell Tuttle. What's that about the tyre?'

'It's flat.'

'What a day!' he exclaimed.

He began to get undressed.

'A 220-volt line does not account for thumps, knocks and crashes.'

'There are chipmunks all over here. They can get in the walls of old houses and cause a lot of damage.'

'It wasn't chipmunks.'

'Or,' he yawned, 'bats. Anyone who smashed into a parked car, takes ten minutes to make a putt, and cheats on his score, would, in my opinion, inherit a house with bats in the belfry.'

'It wasn't bats.'

He climbed into bed. 'Furthermore,' he went on, delivering the clincher, 'he's got to be crazy. Sits in the clubhouse eating fruit salad and doesn't see the girls go by.' He gave me a reassuring pat. 'Not a leg to compare with yours.' He yawned again. 'Better come next time though. A man can get distracted with someone like that.' His voice was getting sleepier. 'Look at all this trouble you got us into with this cleaning fru for aw.'

'It wasn't fru for aw. They weren't chipmunks. It wasn't bats. It was a nail . . .' But he was pretending, or he had fallen asleep. I was not satisfied. I lay awake and listened, remembering how it had been when we first had come here – the lazy days by the pond, the moonlit nights. The rest of the summer stretched ahead – ideal for two, not three. What had happened to Sam?

The steps were measured and plain as they climbed up from the cellar and crossed the house down the hall to our bedroom. As if a hat were pulled off the bedpost, there was a slithering sound followed by a sharp crack and *Hunt and Fish* fell off the night table. I squeezed Jay's arm, but he did not stir and the steps moved away and over the living-room floor. A draught reached across the room to us, as with a click the front door opened. Was it Sam? I had to know. Tiptoeing down the hall, I peered around the corner. His right arm encircling the pot of ivy, Sam was waiting in the doorway.

With one last furious pitch, he hurled it across the room at me, but his curve ball was out of practice and it fell just short of my feet. Awakened by the crash, Jay appeared at my side.

'Sam has gone,' I said.

Jay put his arm around me. 'Better stick close to Papa,' he murmured. 'He might come back. Remember what Tuttle said. "You had to watch out for Sam."'

But I was certain that Sam was on his way to find Myra. The way I figured it, when I moved his things, Sam got mad. He had been so comfortable down there, that until I shot him, and square between the eyes, Sam did not know that he was dead.

28 TOWER STREET

Duncan Forbes

The house was due to be demolished in six months, but our landlord, Mr Scott, still ran his gents' hairdressing business on the ground floor even though Eileen's Ladies' Hairdressing had already moved from its salon on the first floor. Simon and I had a bedroom each on the second and top floor, with our kitchen and living-room down in the basement. Our rent was remarkably low for such spacious furnished accommodation in Oxford, and so I considered it excellent luck when Simon asked me to share it with him after his intended flatmate from his own College had left Oxford for a year off.

Lizzy, on the other hand, disliked 28 Tower Street from the start because it was so primitive. It had no bathroom, and the basement was damp. The bedrooms were three floors above the basement and the outside lavatory, but it had better cooking facilities than Lizzy's bedsit. So we slept at 28 Tower Street and had baths at her place or in College. Lizzy was a Modern Linguist from St Hugh's and I was reading English at John's. I was immediately attracted to Lizzy by her vivacity and her wit, by her big brown eyes and her long straight brown hair which she periodically made me beg her to keep growing.

The evening before Simon arrived, I returned late to find my door key wouldn't turn in the lock. I tried lifting the door up fractionally by the doorhandle, but the key still wouldn't turn. I knocked irritably on the door and rattled it by the handle. Finally, I rang Lizzy's bicycle bell, or rather I made it give a series of whirring pings.

No lights had gone on in the house, but Lizzy suddenly opened the door and rushed out. She was obviously extremely scared. She had difficulty telling me what was wrong and I had trouble persuading her back into the house. The meter had run out, so we went downstairs together by the light of her bike lamp and I put a 10p piece in the meter.

Apparently Lizzy had been reading in bed when she heard some youths belching and singing outside in Tower Street.

As it was just after closing time, she decided for safety's sake to put the catch down on the front door, and then she went back to bed. Within five minutes the lights in the house went out. Until she realized that the meter had run out, this had worried Lizzy. But when she couldn't find the 10p piece which she was sure she had in her purse, she became uncontrollably frightened. She dressed and decided to walk to meet me, when suddenly she heard footsteps coming up the stairs. She was convinced they were a man's, but she was sure they weren't mine. The man whistled a Mozart concerto perfectly in tune for about a minute and then the noise just stopped. The man did not appear to go away. For five minutes there was complete silence until I knocked on the door. Privately I thought her fears were entirely corny, prompted by such spooky clichés as the empty house, the nearby church, which had some recently reopened graves, and the locked and deserted first floor. All it needed was Wolf Mankiewicz and his Orchestra locked away in Eileen's empty Ladies' Hairdressing Salon on the first floor to play some suitably sepulchral chords, and the place would be an ideal set for a horror film, I thought. So I tried to persuade Lizzy that it could simply have been someone next door coming upstairs whistling. But she was certain he had been on our stairs. She was too frightened to imitate the man's whistling or even hum the tune for me, and later that night she refused to go downstairs to the outside lavatory without me as an escort.

I thought that the following morning Lizzy would try to insist on sleeping at her place, but the prospect of Simon's arrival that day seemed to reassure her. This was strange because as far as I knew she had met him only once.

Simon was reading Law at Oriel, having switched from Classics. He was tall, fair-haired, and wore mainly dung-coloured sports jackets, trousers and shoes. He had spent an unenjoyable year between Wellington and Oxford on VSO in Kenya as a schoolteacher, and his room already contained a tribal mask and some other Kenyan mementoes, along with his golf clubs and squash racket. I had taken a liking to him when I first met him because he had successfully pretended to be the Oriel College chaplain.

When I came back from the Bodleian for lunch, Simon was already in the basement eating scrambled egg on toast. We said how pleased we were to see each other again and while I put two eggs on to boil, we told each other what we had done over the summer. During our lunch, I told Simon about the skeletons discovered the day before in the trench outside and I described the whistling man Lizzy claimed to have heard the previous night.

'But you weren't here?' he asked.

'No.'

'And it just came upstairs whistling?'

'Apparently.'

'It's all those graves being opened by the Public Works Department. Couldn't fail to work on an impressionable female mind.'

'I tried to explain to her gently that she might be imagining it all.'

'Or else,' Simon suggested, 'it's the ghost of Eileen, late of Ladies' Hairdressing.'

'Who whistled while she gave her clients a Baskerville back-comb.'

'Or the tuneful whistling of the drill of Dracula's dentist.'

'Or a werewolf whistle.'

'Or Wolfgang Amadeus himself.'

'Come back in vain to get Eileen to perm his wig.'

'Eileen's Poltergeist Perm,' said Simon triumphantly.

So we christened the ghost Eileen, and Simon said he would wake me if he ever heard her. Before I left, he asked me to buy him a round-pin plug for his tape-recorder, as I was going past the electrician's.

That evening, Lizzy cooked us a moussaka and Simon brought two pints of mild in a jug from the pub over the road from the church. We all went to bed at about 11.30 after studying during the evening. We heard Simon get out of bed and switch his light out before we switched out ours. I had been lying awake for about half an hour when I heard Simon going downstairs. I listened again. No, the footsteps sounded like Simon's but they were coming upstairs. I immediately felt panicky. I lay rigid and listened intently. Above the sound of my shallow breathing, I could hear someone whistling Mozart loud and in tune. I waited. My heart was beating fast. The whistling and the footsteps drew closer.

I have often wondered what I would do at such a crisis. How I would talk to a suicide, pacify a strangler, react to Lizzy disfigured in a car crash, cope with a corpse, or face any violent death myself. I raised my head stiffly off the pillow and stared at the door. The doorhandle gleamed slightly orange where it caught the street lighting. The door opened. A figure stood in the doorway carrying a tall sort of walking stick. I remember my sole reaction well. I neither screamed, nor spoke, as I had imagined I would. I whimpered. Then I heard the figure whisper:

'Eileen.' It was Simon. 'Come on,' he said. I sat up pretending to have been aroused from a deep sleep.

'Quick,' said Simon.

I rolled out of bed and followed Simon out. He had a golf club in his hand. We crept down the stairs. The lino was cold under my bare feet. I could still hear the whistling. Although the footsteps had stopped, I could understand now why Lizzy had been so frightened the night before. Simon stopped on the first landing in front of me. I saw him peering intently into the dark outside Eileen's. Then he joined in the Mozart. He whistled in tune and time for a few bars. I couldn't tell what he was up to when he ceased to whistle, lunged forward with his golf club and swiped at the thick air outside Eileen's door. The other whistling stopped.

'Get a torch,' he said without turning round. I fetched Lizzy's bike lamp from our bedroom and switched it on gratefully for my return journey of five yards. Simon squinted into the lamp beam. I gave him the lamp and he shone it at the door of Eileen's. The bright circle travelled over the cream gloss paint of the door. Then Simon walked down the stairs and tried to open the door. It was still locked.

'I'm going outside into the street to see if I can see anything there.'

'OK,' I said. 'I'll stay here.'

He took the golf club and bike lamp with him and went downstairs softly. I noticed he was wearing crepe-soled shoes. He must have put them on as soon as he heard the whistling.

Or else – but yes, why not? It suddenly occurred to me that Simon was playing a practical joke on us. As this was a less frightening belief than that there was a real intruder in the house at that moment, I tried to work out Simon's actions. He must have waited till he heard us switch out our light, then he must have put on his shoes, crept downstairs and simply walked upstairs again, whistling Mozart. So that was why he'd wanted a plug on his tape-recorder so badly. He'd needed to rehearse his Mozart. But then I thought I'd heard two of them whistling at once, although I might well have been wrong.

At that point in my inner debate, I suddenly heard someone behind me. My argument instantly collapsed. I should never have stayed on the stairs. I had no torch and no weapon. But it was Lizzy who said:

'What is it?' and she sounded worried too.

'It's him.'

'Who?'

'Your whistler.'

'Where?'

'I don't know.'

I explained that Simon had gone outside to investigate and imagined it was him we could hear coming back up the stairs now.

'Why's he whistling then?' Lizzy asked.

I listened carefully. There was someone on the landing below us outside Eileen's again.

Then for the first time he started up the two short flights towards our bedroom. He was still whistling Mozart as casually as ever, although the stairs appeared to have made him a little short of breath, as the whistling was less fluent. Lizzy backed away and tried to tug me with her. I stayed. I could see the dark outline of the man now against the darker blur of the wallpaper. As he turned to face me up the last flight of stairs, I was suddenly blinded by a flash of light in my face. I ducked out of its glare. Should I speak to him? Or should I rush to Lizzy in our bedroom and barricade us in? The man turned the torch slowly through ninety degrees so that the bright circle travelled from my face up our bedroom door, on to the ceiling and along until it glowed on his features ghoulishly from below. His head would have looked like an exhibit from the Chamber of Horrors if I hadn't recognized whose it was. Even so, his smile was an oddly sinister sneer in the light of the bike lamp.

'Good God!' I said.

'No. Me.' It was Simon.

'I thought so,' he said.

'Thought what?'

'You're afraid of ghosts and so you believe in them. I've just proved it. You were scared stiff.'

'So would you have been.'

'I wasn't. I went downstairs.'

I shrugged. 'Ah, but it was all right for you. You knew it wasn't a ghost or even anyone else.'

'How could I?'

'You went downstairs and came up imitating the ghost Lizzy told me about.'

'Not the first time. That wasn't me.'

'You expect me to believe that now?' I shouted.

Lizzy had come out on to the landing because she could hear us arguing. Instead of joining in on my side against Simon as I naturally expected she would, she rounded on me.

'Did you tell Simon what happened to me here last night?' she demanded.

'Yes. Shouldn't I have?'

'It didn't occur to you that I might not like you to talk about the things I hear.'

'Well, I wish I hadn't told him now. He's been posing as your ghost.'

'It wasn't me the first time,' Simon said indignantly.

'Well, you did a very good imitation of yourself second time up the stairs, in that case,' I pointed out.

'Why do the impersonation at all?' Lizzy asked.

'Because I don't believe in ghosts and I'm not frightened of fallacies.'

'Well, now you've had your cheap thrill, let's get back to bed,' I said.

'Look,' Simon said firmly, 'I want to find out who it is that's whistling just as much as you.'

'Sure.'

'I do, really. So, why don't we set a trap for it tomorrow?

We'll wait up for Eileen on a rota. Right? Half the night each, unless Lizzy wants to take a turn. No? OK. And we try and tape-record her on my machine.'

'You better get busy with your sound effects then. All you need do is make a tape of footsteps and whistled Mozart and then play it to us, first for the ghost and then as proof.'

'Well, don't bother if you don't want to. But I'm interested in this. It would be better if you were a damn sight more sceptical of ghosts and less sceptical of me.'

With that, we all went back to bed, and before we went to sleep Lizzy attacked me once again for telling Simon about the things she'd heard. I argued that Simon might resent her presence in the flat since he had no girl-friend at that time, and I said he might be using Eileen as a ploy to get her not to sleep in the flat. But that still didn't account for the noises Lizzy had heard. It occurred to me then, although I didn't mention it, that Lizzy might somehow be in league with Simon. But, if so, her simulation of fright the previous night had been remarkably authentic.

The next day was a Sunday. It was quiet outside except when the predominantly undergraduate congregation of St Ebbe's came for Family Communion on their bicycles and left after coffee in the crypt. I told Simon I would watch for Eileen from 12 till 4 a.m. I resented my reputation with him as a gullible and irrational coward, and I wanted to prove that even if I had my fears I could conquer them. On top of that, I preferred to live at 28 Tower Street rather than at Lizzy's bedsit and so I wanted to exorcize Eileen's ghost. Finally, there was a Norman Davis lecture on the language of 'The Nun's Preeste's Tale at 10 a.m. on Mondays and I welcomed the excuse to miss it. But I told Simon that I would watch for only one night.

Lizzy thought we were both mad as she was now convinced that Simon was using the pretext of the ghost to frighten her out of the house. She suspected I was colluding with Simon in some way and in retaliation took herself off to her bedsit for the night.

I got ready for my vigil (at 11.30 p.m.). Simon showed me

how to work his tape-recorder and we arranged the flex and lead at their full extents so that the microphone reached almost to Eileen's landing. I put my pyjamas on under my clothes, and wore rugger socks, two jerseys and Simon's overcoat for extra warmth. He lent me his number 7 iron as a weapon. Neither of our bedroom doors locked and we therefore arranged the beds so that we could barricade the doors in the shortest possible time. I took Lizzy's bike lamp and chose two detested overweight books as ammunition: Klaeber's edition of *Beowulf* and *Milton's Poetical Works*, ed. Carey & Fowler. We had agreed not to read in order to save torchlight and I knew I would be tempted by neither of those tomes. Simon set his alarm for 3.55, closed his door and went to bed. The three bars of light around his door soon vanished and I was left alone in the dark.

I counted as St Ebbe's Church clock chimed midnight. I had positioned myself next to Simon's tape-recorder on the small landing directly overlooking the entrance to Eileen's. I could see the top of the tape-recorder gleaming and I felt the keyboard so that I knew I could press the right switch if necessary. I positioned Simon's golf club so that I could grab it rapidly without knocking it downstairs. As I was doing so, I heard a noise like a gramophone needle scratching a radius on an LP. It seemed to be coming from our garden. I looked out of the window. The house cast a shadow over its garden of flowering cabbage and unmown hay. But I saw a cat leap on to and over the garden wall and presumed I must have heard it scratching. I sat down again to watch.

Out of fear, boredom, cold or a mixture of all three, I soon felt the need to go to the outside lavatory. I took the bike lamp with me and brought myself up a cup of coffee. Simon was waiting for me on the top landing. I whistled a few bars of Mozart's 'Minuet in D' at him to pay him back.

'Everything all right?' he asked.

'Fine,' I answered, and he went back to bed. As it happened, I did not have to budge again during my watch. St Ebbe's chimed the hours and the half-hours, while I watched and waited, wishing that I smoked, or chewed gum, or could read. I tried to 'think', but the thought that kept on emerging was that a university education does not equip one's thought processes to entertain one in the small hours. Both my legs went dead at one time or another and I had to massage their tingling bulk back to life.

When Simon's alarm went, I was greatly relieved. At first I had found the problem fear, then it was boredom, but now it was fatigue and discomfort. I longed to go to bed and I suggested Simon did the same. I could see no point in his spending the rest of the night out there, I said, because Eileen usually only came at about midnight. But Simon insisted and I was too tired to object. So I gave him back his coat, said good night to him and went to bed. I did nevertheless make the obvious mental note that Eileen hadn't appeared while Simon had been safe in his room and while I had been able to observe his movements.

I must have gone to sleep almost immediately and I imagine I slept heavily, because I don't remember anything till I was woken at 8.10 a.m. when the road drill started gunning outside. Once I had realized it was Monday morning, I remembered two things apart from a dream about railways: our watch for Eileen, and the Norman Davis lecture. I decided to check with Simon about Eileen and then go back to bed and miss the lecture as planned.

When I saw Simon, I was disgusted by his lack of stamina. I went quietly back into my bedroom and reset my alarm for three minutes' time. Simon was leaning awkwardly against the wall with his eyes closed. I'll watch him wake up, I thought, putting my alarm clock on the stair above him. I stood back so that I could see him through the banisters. I started to examine Simon critically in an attempt to explain to myself why he appeared to have no girl-friends, when I realized that the tape-recorder beside him had gone. He couldn't be leaning over it. There was simply no room, and the lead no longer ran to his bedroom. I had half expected that the tape-recorder would be tampered with during Simon's watch, but I couldn't understand why it needed to be removed. I went down the stairs to investigate.

Simon still had beside him his golf club, my books and an ashtray with ash scattered round it so that it looked like a spent Mount Vesuvius Indoor Firework. Simon himself looked ill. I shook him by the shoulder, then I called his name. Normally he was first up in the mornings, so I didn't know what he was like to wake up. Then I saw for the first time that part of his forehead and scalp were purple as if they had suddenly acquired a blackcurrant stain. I couldn't believe it. I parted his hair and at the roots the aubergine skin made me retch. I think I realized then for the first time that he might be dead. My alarm went off idiotically and I stopped it as soon as I could. All I could think of to do for Simon was prompted by memories of fiction or of Boy Scout First Aid manuals. I bent down and listened to his heart, but my ear didn't register anything through the thick warmth of his coat. I felt for his pulse. His wrist was cold, but I could feel a faint blip although I didn't know if it was his or mine. So, as they do in war films, I lifted one of his eyelids, not really knowing what to look for. But as soon as I had I knew he was dead. Only half his blue iris was visible, the white was bloodshot, and it looked as if his eye socket had tried to swallow his eyeball whole. His eyeball looked like a gobstopper on the white change layer between blue and red. I let the eyelid go and to my horror it stayed up, so that Simon seemed to be giving me a supremely exasperated wink.

I dressed and ran as fast as I could to the telephone box down the road. I told the duty police constable I thought Simon had been killed and gave our address. I waited outside until the police had arrived. I didn't want to go back into the house on my own. I didn't know how to explain why Simon had been sitting on the stairs from four to eight in the morning. I made up my mind just to tell the truth. Two police cars arrived and Simon was confirmed dead. A police photographer was called for and I was taken to the police station at St Aldate's.

I could not stop myself thinking of that massive bruise and the dead eye. The sight of them both kept coming back to me again and again, but despite this I still couldn't believe Simon was dead. I could tell that the police thought my talk about a ghost we called Eileen was undergraduate frivolity compared to the murder, query suicide, query query accidental death of Simon Robert Antony Holder, 20, which they were investigating and on whose body they had ordered an autopsy and report.

'If it was a ghost who killed your friend,' I remember the detective saying, 'he still had more than a finger in the land of the living, because he stole 200 Park Drive and three-pound-odd petty cash from the gents' hairdresser's down below you, and well as Mr Holder's tape-recorder. No, this is manslaughter, if you ask me.'

I tried to keep this in mind when I went back to 28 Tower Street that evening to fetch some of my things. I had been at the police station all day and I was tired and shocked. I wanted to pack a case and go over to Lizzy's as quickly as I could. As soon as I went into the house, I switched on every possible light including those in the basement. I carefully avoided treading where Simon's corpse had been. My bedroom was cold and so I switched on the fire. I was fetching a change of clothes to pack when I realized that Lizzy's clothes and books had gone. I wondered why and decided that this either meant desertion of me, or was because of Simon's murder which she might somehow have heard about. But I would find out which when I saw her. I was just about to go down to the basement to fetch my wash-things and was thinking that I didn't like the prospect of leaving any dark rooms behind me, when all the lights in the house went out.

A miserable panic overtook me. I searched desperately for Lizzy's bike lamp but couldn't find it anywhere. The electric fire ticked as it cooled. I thought I might take my case as it was and dash for the front door. What I dreaded was to hear the whistling again, or be attacked. Once I had made that clear to myself I felt I could face the irrationality of my fears. I felt in my pockets for change so that I could set the meter spinning again just once more, but I only had coppers. Then I saw the black bike lamp on my bed. I have rarely felt more relieved. I picked it up and switched it on. The light flickered and the beam was yellower than when I had last used it, but it still worked.

I took my case and stood outside Simon's bedroom door. I wondered if he had had any change I could use for the meter. After all, I thought callously, although I welcomed the thought because it was callous, if he'd put his share in the meter, the lights wouldn't be out now. With the thought of Simon, however, the memories of his bloodshot eye and his purple forehead flashed momentarily before my eyes. I turned round to check the hostile dark behind me and opened Simon's bedroom door.

I flashed the bike lamp round the room. It lit up the familiar golf clubs, bookcase, tribal mask, wardrobe and desk. There was no loose change on top of his desk and so I decided to frisk a jacket of Simon's which was hanging over a chair. The right-hand pocket clinked and felt heavy, but it contained only a bicycle padlock and chain. I was putting this lock back in the pocket when I thought I heard a noise from somewhere else in the house. It might just have been a sound from next door, but I held my breath and listened, feeling wretchedly unworthy of any new ordeal.

Instead of the silence I had hoped to hear, there was definitely someone coming up the stairs. Panicking, I tried to work out who it might reasonably be; Lizzy, perhaps, or the police again. But then between each footstep, between each unfeminine scuff of shoe on lino, I could pick out low, tuneful whistling. That whistling was what I had dreaded most. It made me feel cold and defenceless. My scalp tingled and I shuddered jerkily. I shone the bike lamp at the dingy wallpaper down the top flight of stairs and called out feebly, 'Who's there?' There was no answer. There was not even a pause in the footsteps or the whistling, which grew louder as they approached the jaundiced circle of torchlight.

I backed slowly into the dark of Simon's bedroom. Whoever it was whistling clearly knew the way up because there was no hesitation in his footsteps. I waited with only my pathetic toy searchlight flickering between me and the doorway. I pushed the switch over to 'on' as hard as I could in an effort to squeeze more light out of the lamp. I could feel my heart trying to kick down my ribcage and I wished I hadn't called out. If only I hadn't asked who was there, perhaps he would have gone away. Then I saw him. He was standing in the doorway, still wearing the clothes he had died in, and he was grinning so much he could hardly keep whistling his Mozart.

For an instant I wanted to believe it was all part of an elaborate hoax once again, but as I started to scream, Simon vanished and I knew then that it was real and that if I could only scream without stopping I might be safe. I must have run down the stairs and out on to the street, as I was found, still hysterical, by three Catt's men who took me to the Radcliffe Infirmary, thinking I must have had a bad trip.

But I am sure now it was Simon's ghost that I had seen, that we had all heard, and that he himself had never believed in.

THE GREY COTTAGE

Mrs Claxton

The cottage was old and grey. A pear tree ran over the front of it; there was a wooden porch covered with jessamine and honeysuckle, which promised to be very sweet and delightful in the spring. It stood in a pretty garden, sloping down to a thick hedge; beyond this, and much below it, ran the lane leading up into the village. A large walnut tree and some tall fir trees shaded the cottage to the south; while the hill, on the side of which it was built, protected it from the north winds: they blew keenly enough at times. An orchard divided us from our neighbours at the back; from the front we looked over the thatched roofs of a few low dwellings to the wide valley beyond, where a lazy river wound in and out through clumps of pollards. A picturesque mill and loch lay to the left; to the right a graceful spire rose in the distance.

Such was my new home. It was chosen partly for its retirement and its pretty garden, chiefly on account of its low rental and the inexpensive neighbourhood. The nearest town was three miles off; more than that when the floods were out, as was often the case, for then the short cut across the fields was impassable.

This Grey Cottage – called so, possibly, from the old greystone of which it was built – had belonged to an aged man of the name of Vallyer. He had purchased it some fifty years before. By nature, as we heard, he had been close and miserly, saving up by little and little until he was reputed to be very rich. His wife he lost shortly after their marriage; and since that time he had led a most solitary life, the only other inmate of the cottage being an aged housekeeper, very deaf, and as eccentric as himself. Occasionally a married sister would come over to spend a few hours with him, but never stayed over the night. These visits were like angels' in being few and far between; but in another respect very unlike angels', for they never took place without a quarrel, and a declaration on the part of the sister, Mrs Bittern, that she would never enter the house again. People said her only reason for making these quarrels up, was the old man's money. Be that as it might, virtue proved to be its own reward, for when he died it was found he had left her nothing.

The old gentleman was wonderfully fond of his garden, working in it the greater part of the day, and seldom going beyond it. It was strange that with all his love for his flowers, he should never have cared to show them to his neighbours. On the contrary, he did what he could to keep them from their sight. During his life the place was unknown land; and, consequently, the subject of much curiosity, especially to the village children. Mr Vallyer always seemed to be on the look-out if they attempted to peer and pry through the hedge or over the gate, and he carried a thick stick, with which he would make sudden lunges and thrusts, scattering the young visitors ignominiously. It was not safe for juvenile eyes to gaze into Mr Vallyer's property. Another peculiarity he had. It was to stand by the garden gate in the gloaming leaning on his stick, and watching the few people who went up and down the lonely lane. No matter what the night was, under the bright frosty stars of winter, or in the mist following a heated day of summer, there would stand old Michael Vallyer.

It has been said that he was supposed to have saved money. None – save a few pounds – could be found after his death. It then became known that he had purchased a life annuity, which had died with him. The cottage and furniture were left to a nephew, a chemist in London. Not requiring to live in it himself, he advertised it to be let furnished. Two maiden ladies had taken it first by the month; but they had quickly given notice to leave, complaining of damp and other disagreeables. They had, however, always been considered rather crotchety people. I, with my two pretty nieces, Hilda and Cecily, took possession at Michaelmas, a few weeks after they left. We were pleased with our country home. The few neighbours were friendly and sociable. I began to look upon the little Grey Cottage as a haven of rest after a changeful and troubled life.

As our old servant, Martha, was not quite as active as she used to be, I enquired for a charwoman, to come in twice a week to assist her, and was recommended to a Mrs Briggs. She did not do her work amiss, but her propensity to gossip was irrepressible.

'You should see the place in the spring, ma'am, when the gillyflowers and stocks is out,' she said to me one day, when I was in the kitchen making a tart, and she stood at the other end of it cleaning brasses and tins. 'It looked beautiful when the Miss Jessops first came here.'

'I wonder what made them leave so soon?' I remarked. 'Damp, the agent told me: but I have discovered no damp about the cottage.'

'It weren't the damp, ma'am,' was Mrs Briggs's answer, and I thought her tone significant. 'At first they liked it – oh, so much: but in a little time they said they must leave. Doubtless,' lowering her voice, 'the ladies had their reasons.'

'Perhaps they found it too lonely?'

'No, and it weren't exactly the loneliness,' returned Mrs Briggs. 'Not that altogether, ma'am.'

I asked no more; for gossip, though Mrs Briggs's chief failing, is not one of mine; but went on with my pastry-making. She, rubbing fiercely at the copper tea-kettle, began again after an interlude.

'Did you chance to hear nothing about this cottage, ma'am?'

'Nothing particular. Why? What is there to hear?'

'Perhaps I ought not to tell it you, ma'am; you might be scared,' returned she, as she looked at me over the kettle.

'Scared! Not I. Pray tell what you have to tell – if it concerns the cottage.'

'Well, ma'am, it's a healthy place and a pretty place; that's for sure. But – it's about the old gentleman.'

'The old gentleman!'

'Old Mr Vallyer. They say he is in the house.'

'Why, what do you mean?' I asked, feeling somewhat as the woman had said – scared.

'It's said, ma'am, that he never went out of it, though his funeral did; that he stopped in to haunt it. Folks talk of something that happened here years and years ago; some friend of Mr Vallyer's came from over the seas to visit him. They used to quarrel, and one night the stranger was found dead in the garden. Some thought the death didn't come about by accident; that Vallyer knew more than he said. Anyway, it's pretty sure he can't rest now, but is about the place troubling it.'

I am not especially superstitious, but I confess I did not

like the tale. Mrs Briggs continued. Her tongue, once oiled, would have gone on for ever.

'The first to see him was the Widow Munn's children; he had been dead about a month. I was at her place, helping her with a day's washing. "Mother," said they, running in at dusk, "we have seen the old gentleman at the Grey Cottage; he's leaning over the gate with his stick just as he used to be." They weren't frightened, those young children; they told it as a bit of news. The Widow Munn looked at me, and I at her, and then she whipped 'em all round, thinking it might be the best way to put it out of their heads.'

I laughed; and said the children might have been mistaken.

'So they might, ma'am,' assented Mrs Briggs. 'The next to see it was a stranger: a young man coming through the village one moonlight night on his way to London; he was walking it. He went into the public-house, down there in Greenford, and called for a glass of ale. While he was sitting by the fire drinking it, he began to talk. "What uncivil people you seem to have in these parts," says he. "I asked an old gentleman, standing at his garden gate half-way up the hill, whether there was a public-house near, and he would not answer me; he just stared straight in my face with his glassy-looking eyes, and never spoke." The company in the tap-room stopped talking at this, and looked at one another. "What sort of an old gentleman was it?" they asked; "how was he dressed?"

'"He wore a long grey coat, with a curious little cape to it," says the traveller, "and a spotted white kerchief, tied loose round his neck, with the ends hanging, and he had a stick in his hand. *Very* civil, I must say he was! I asked him the question again in a louder tone, thinking he might be deaf; but he never answered, only continued to stare at me." It was the dress of old Vallyer, ma'am; he never wore any other, and I'll leave you to judge what the company at the White Hart thought of it. A deal of talk went about Greenford next day.'

'Where is the old maid-servant?'

'She went away. They left her in the house to show it, but after a week or two she took the key to the agent, saying there was something she did not like about the place, and she shouldn't stop in it. Just before the Miss Jessops took it, that was.'

'No wonder the Miss Jessops were frightened away from the cottage if such tales were told to them,' I remarked. 'Why, you Greenford people must have driven them away!'

'Ah, well, I see, ma'am, you don't believe in it. It was said the ladies saw him in the house as well as out of it, though I can't speak for certain as to what happened. They went away all quiet and composed like; they didn't want to be laughed at.'

We found that Mr Vallyer's ghost was firmly believed in by the neighbourhood. Fortunately my nieces were sensible girls, and only laughed. The stories told were made a source of amusement to them, and their young friends. They treated the subject as a good joke; sometimes intruding irreverently near the confines of that strange and mysterious world beyond whose veil we know so little, and which, it has always seemed to me, should be treated with respect, if not with awe. On one occasion I felt obliged to expostulate.

'Why, Aunt Cameron,' exclaimed Hilda, laughing, 'I am almost sure you believe in the ghost!'

Cecily took the matter more seriously, and agreed with me that too much fun had been made. After that, it was a favourite joke of Hilda's to tell her friends confidentially that her aunt and Cecily believed in old Vallyer's reappearance.

Weeks passed away, during which we saw nothing, and the winter set in. A young nephew of mine, and cousin to my nieces, came to spend some days with us; chiefly, I believe, on account of the skating. His arrival made Hilda and Cecily think it high time to make a little return for the kindness and hospitality which had been shown to us; or, rather, to induce me to think it. I let myself be persuaded, and cards went out for a small evening party.

The weather was now intensely cold. The river had been flooded before the frost set in; not only that, but also the meadows were frozen over. We might almost have been at the North Pole, such an expanse of snow and ice did we overlook. The village seemed skating mad; and, not content with the day's amusement, our young people would remain on the ice until late at night, for the moon, nearing the full, shone brilliantly in a cloudless sky.

Leonard, my nephew, was a clever and amusing young

fellow, holding strong views on many subjects, and propounding them with all the energy and decision of youth and inexperience. Old customs and old beliefs were not good enough for him – 'nous avons changé tout cela' was his motto. I do not think he really believed, or rather disbelieved, all he pretended to do. He liked to startle us, and delighted in shocking the prejudices of his cousins, especially of Hilda, who was a warm partisan of that very ultra school of theology which is now so prevalent amongst the young and imaginative. On one point, however, they both agreed – a strong disbelief in the supernatural.

The evening of the party arrived, and brought our guests. Sixteen in all, including our own young people; I made the seventeenth. The time passed pleasantly, and lastly dancing was introduced. They had had a few quadrilles, when one gentleman had to leave, to catch a midnight train: and when a double set of Lancers was formed after his departure, one was lacking to make it up. There were only fifteen. You may think it strange I should enter into such particulars, but you will see.

'You must do double duty, Leonard,' I said.

'No, Aunt,' exclaimed Hilda, with a saucy smile. 'You shall invite old Mr Vallyer to join us. I wish he would!'

All laughed; and then our neighbour, Mrs Goldsmith, a tall, handsome woman, called out that she had no objection to dance with the old gentleman – should like to. 'See, here he is!' she went on, making a bow to the sofa cushion in her careless merriment, and taking it up in her arms. 'You are not accustomed to dancing, sir, so we will go to the side. Now let us begin.'

I had been so used to playing dance music, that I did it quite mechanically, often turning half round on the music stool to watch the dancers while my fingers were busy. My nieces were fine-looking girls, and I liked to follow Hilda's striking figure and Cecily's quiet grace as they moved through the mazes of the dance. After striking up the first inspiriting chords of the Lancers, I turned to see how Mrs Goldsmith was getting on with her 'partner'. She stood opposite to Cecily and young Kirby, a rising engineer, with whom she was dancing. Hilda and Leonard were at the bottom of the set.

There was a good deal of laughing at the cushion at first,

but it soon subsided, and I was glad of it, for I had fatigued myself much in preparing for our little entertainment; my head ached now, and the mirth jarred upon my nerves. I began to feel in that stage of weariness when voices sound far off; when the hands work on at whatever occupies them, without help from the brain; when the thoughts roam away and the eye sees things mistily. It suddenly struck me that the room was growing very cold. Just as Mrs Goldsmith was passing me, cushion in arm, I felt a shiver.

'Ten degrees below freezing point last night, and colder tonight,' I thought to myself. 'What shall we come to?'

Turning round again to look at the dancing, I noticed how very pale they appeared, and how singularly quiet. Why had they ceased talking? As Cecily glided past me, I was struck by her face. It was white as marble, and her blue eyes were strangely distended and fixed with a puzzled kind of fascination on Mrs Goldsmith. Mine followed them. That lady was moving through the figure in her stately manner, the cushion still in her arms, and a fixed smile on her lips; and by her side – now, was it an overwrought brain or was I dreaming? Surely the latter, for I felt no surprise, no alarm – *there danced by her side a little old man!*

Everything seemed in a mist now, as though the night were foggy, and the fog had got into the room, so I could not see the stranger clearly. The music sounded muffled, and my thoughts went back to former nights in London, when the thick yellow vapour enveloped the streets, and link boys were out, and conductors led omnibuses, and people shouted with hollow voices. It seemed hours since I began to play that set of Lancers.

This old man was dressed in a long grey coat, with a little cape, and a white spotted neckerchief loosely tied, and he carried a thick stick in his hand. He danced in an old-world fashion, executing his steps with great precision, and making formal bows to his partner and the rest of the company. Just then Mrs Goldsmith laid the cushion back on the sofa; shivering apparently with cold, she took up a scarf and wrapped it closely round her, dancing all the time. It was now the grand chain in the last figure, and for a moment or two I lost sight of the old man. Suddenly there was a wild scream – the dance stopped – Cecily had fainted!

A medical man, Mr Brook, was of the party. He attributed Cecily's attack to the intense coldness of the weather, and to the morning's skating, when she must have over-fatigued herself. The depression most of them had felt during the last set of quadrilles he put down to the same cause – unusual cold.

Cecily continued very poorly the following day. She confided to me privately her extraordinary impressions of the previous evening. I found them to be similar to my own; but I mentioned nothing to her about myself, and laughed a little.

'But I did see the old man, Aunt Cameron,' she persisted. 'He was by Mrs Goldsmith's side.'

I would not listen. On the contrary, I treated the matter entirely from a common-sense point of view; endeavouring to persuade her that the whole thing was due to an overwrought imagination. Indeed I was by no means sure that such was not the case. It was more likely that our brains, hers and mine, should have worked in the same groove, been 'en rapport', as the mesmerists would have expressed it, than that we should really have seen an apparition. We are all aware of those invisible magnetic wires which so often flash a message from one brain to another, those mysterious reminders which at times precede the arrival of an absent friend – the dream at night followed by the letter of the morrow. 'There are,' as Hamlet hath it, 'more things in heaven and earth than are dreamt of in our philosophy.' What we call the supernatural may be but the gleams of a hidden science some time to be revealed.

Cecily tried to take up my view of the case. We agreed not to mention the matter to Hilda, or to anyone else.

'Please, Mr Cameron, you are wanted,' said Martha to my nephew, interrupting us that same evening when we were all sitting together, young Kirby, the engineer, being with us.

'Who is it?' cried Leonard.

'Will you please come out, sir; he won't give any name.'

Leonard went out. He came back again in a minute or two, and beckoned to Kirby, who was playing chess with Hilda.

'It's nothing,' he said, as we all started up. 'Only Martha has been frightened at someone standing at the back door and then going away without speaking. We'll go round the garden to make sure no tramps are about.'

I left the room myself, thinking of tramps, and of nothing else. The cottage was so low and so covered by fruit trees and trellis that it would have been a very easy matter to climb into the bedrooms. My window, just over the porch, had especial facilities that way, and I went up to it. Opening the lattice very gently, I concealed myself behind the curtain and looked out. The moon was bright. The voices of the two young men reached me from below.

'It's queer, Kirby – after all the talk, you know. Martha says she opened the door to get some wood, and there the old man stood. She thought it was a real tramp, mind you, and she did not like his staring in her face and never speaking. I am sure I saw him; he was going round towards the orchard.'

'Very odd!' replied young Kirby. 'I saw him too. He was leaning over the front gate.'

'And, by Jove, there he is now!'

'Where?'

'At the gate.'

'I don't see him!'

'Nor do I now – he's gone.'

Yes, there was no mistake; *I* saw him too from my window; the old man leaning on his stick at the gate, where he used to stand so often in life. Presently the two young men came in, and I went down.

'Have you seen any tramp, Leonard?'

'No, Aunt. Not a tramp.'

'What then? Anything?'

'*A little old man leaning on a stick.*'

'I saw him too, Mrs Cameron,' added Mr Kirby.

'We had better say nothing to the girls,' whispered Leonard.

'No, nor to anyone else, Leonard. The whole place would be astir.'

'What – on account of old Vallyer?'

I nodded. Just then the girls came running out.

'What a long time you have been! Have you found him?'

'Of course not,' Leonard replied. 'He had got clear off: those tramps are cunning. Let us have supper – it's awfully cold!'

This second little episode put me very much out of conceit with my pretty cottage. My nieces had a pressing invitation from Leonard's mother, and were to return with him to London. I thought I would go away somewhere too.

It was the afternoon of the day before Leonard and they were to leave. We had had one heavy fall of snow, and the air was again thick with the feathery flakes. Strangely depressed, both mentally and bodily, I stood alone at the window and looked out over the valley, which lay so still under its great white shroud. At last Cecily came in and stood by me.

'You will be very lonely, Aunt, after we are gone.'

'Aye.' And then we stood in silence.

Suddenly the girl laid her hand on my arm, as though to attract my attention. A chilly draught of wind seemed to blow through the room, raising the hair off my forehead with a pricking sensation.

A feeble, bent figure, leaning heavily on a stick, passed slowly and silently from the door to the other window. A coal falling in the grate, the flame flickered up, showing distinctly the old man whom I had twice before seen!

The apparition, for such I now felt it to be, stood looking out of the window, with a worn, sad expression, such as his face might often have borne in the lonely, loveless life he had chosen for himself. After a moment or two of perfect stillness I could bear it no longer. Springing to the fire I stirred it vigorously; the flames rose up into the chimney and the little room was in a blaze of light.

The old man was gone! Cecily grasped my hands in both her own, for she had seen it too; every trace of the usual bright colour had vanished from her lips and face, and she was trembling from head to foot.

I went up with them the next day, and took old Martha with me. I could not stay in the place any more. The agent was informed of these facts, and he let me off easily, and made no remonstrance; so we thought mine could not have been the first complaint of the sort.

It is said the grey cottage is to be a cottage no longer; that it is to be pulled down. And I sincerely hope it will be.

MOTHER LOVE

Pamela Cleaver

As she walked along the road, Harriet knew that she was worried but she could not remember why. Nor could she remember why she was out on such a cold, wild night. She was on her way home – that much was clear for she recognized the road which led to the cottage near the church where she lived with her daughter Elizabeth and their dog – but where had she come from?

The air was chill and as she walked, the knife-like wind forced her to lean forward against its pressure, slowing her progress. The skeletal branches of the leafless trees leaped and danced; their clatter was the only sound beside the wind's sobbing that she could hear. The dark clouds were torn veils dragged across the sky allowing her only fitful glimpses of the moon through the rips and rents, but there was light enough for her to find her way beside the frost-rimed, wiry hedge.

She trudged towards the haven of her cottage thinking longingly of the blazing fire at which she would warm her bones, aching cold from the winter's night. She thought about Elizabeth and wondered if the girl would have waited up for her. She would have done had it been Elizabeth who was out, but then, Harriet's whole life had been devoted to Elizabeth, to her comfort and her happiness.

She tried again to remember why she was out of doors on such a night – she was not the sort of woman who enjoyed nocturnal walks so she must have had a good reason, but the harder she tried to pin it down, the more it eluded her.

Soon she came to the outskirts of the village. She knew it was late because the cottage windows were dark and blank like sightless eyes. As she began to climb the hill towards the church and home, her steps were slowed even more by the gradient. It seemed to her that she was walking as if she were ploughing through treacle and she felt strangely weary.

As she got closer to the cottage, a sense of urgency developed and her anxiety increased. She became aware that her errand had to do with Elizabeth; she knew she had had a premonition that something was threatening her daughter – that was what was driving her through the night. She tried to hurry but found she could not. Her limbs moved like those of a sleeper in the grip of a terrible dream.

At last she came to the garden gate which swung free on its hinges adding its creaks to the soughing of the wind. Across the lawn under the apple tree where they sometimes took tea in summer, she could see the spaniel Dainty sniffing the ground. She supposed Elizabeth had let him out. The dog looked up at her approach but to her surprise, instead of the exuberant, tail-wagging greeting he usually gave her, he stared at her, one paw raised, and then, letting out a terrified howl, he flattened his ears and ran towards the back of the house, his tail between his legs. She was not unduly perturbed by this; she supposed either that he had not recognized her in the dark or that the wild wind had spooked him.

She went to the front door which was usually left unlocked but to her exasperation she could not lift the latch; her hands seemed ineffectual, they must be numbed by the cold. No matter, she would walk round the side of the house to the sitting-room window where she thought Elizabeth must be for she could see a sliver of golden light.

She stood on the flowerbed below the window and plaintively called her daughter's name – 'Elizabeth, Elizabeth!' – but the wild wind snatched her words away as it keened round the house. She managed to get a toehold on the brick edge below the weather-boarding and, gripping the edge of the sill, she pulled herself up to look into the room through the chink in the carelessly-drawn curtains.

She saw the logs blazing in the fireplace as they had in her mind's eye. The cosy room was suffused in a warm glow from the oil lamp beside the fireplace. An armchair was drawn up close to the fire and sitting in it was a young man whom she had never seen before. On a cushion at his feet sat Elizabeth, leaning against his knees. His hand rested on Elizabeth's hair which glowed like copper in the flickering firelight.

It was a calm enough scene apparently. You might have said it was the epitome of romance, lovers sitting contentedly in the firelight's glow. There seemed to be nothing to agitate the feelings of a mother, even one as devoted and possessive as Harriet, but to her it seemed a tableau of unspeakable horror.

The man whose hand rested on her daughter's head she recognized for what he was – evil, totally evil. She had never thought of herself as clairvoyant before but tonight her perceptions seemed to be strangely heightened. She thought she could see shadowy bloodstains on his hands, a shadowy noose about his neck.

Just then, Elizabeth looked up at the man and gave him a smile of great sweetness and trust. Harriet bit back a scream. There was no doubt in her mind that Elizabeth's lover was, or would be, a murderer. Whether it was that he would kill her daughter or whether Elizabeth would suffer because she had given her love to one who was destined to end upon the gallows, the anguished mother could not tell. She only knew that somehow she had to warn the girl. It was for this that she had been battling against the bitter night.

'Elizabeth, Elizabeth!' she cried, but, as before, the wind snatched her words from her.

She tried to rap on the window. The effort was intense, lifting her hand was like hefting lead; however, she managed it.

The two staccato taps startled Elizabeth who leaped to her feet, staring at the gap in the curtains. The expression on her face was one of horror and alarm and Harriet wondered why it should be so. Why was there no welcome from her daughter?

Suddenly Harriet became conscious of her outward appearance. She looked down at her hand with unbelieving horror. There was no flesh on the framework of her bones, the hand she saw was a skeleton and it was hers! She heard a strangled scream and realized it was she who had cried out.

The shock caused her to loosen her grip on the sill and she felt herself falling backwards. She did not fall just the short distance from the window to the ground, it was a long, slow, tumbling fall as if it were part of a dream, and when the thud came that ended it, the jerk that wakes the sleeper from the dream, Harriet knew where she was and knew that she was in the place where she belonged, her grave. She was sealed into her coffin under the ground.

For the first time that night her spirit was tranquil. She had a sense of achievement; in spite of the immense difficulties implicit in her situation, she had managed to warn Elizabeth – no mother could do more. At last she could rest and turn her thoughts from earthly concerns.

In the cottage, he held Elizabeth in his arms. 'Dear heart, you are trembling. What is the matter – what did you see?'

She buried her head in his shoulder. 'It was horrible, horrible! An apparition – I cannot even talk about it.'

He soothed her as one would a child, saying 'hush' and 'there, there'. He sat down in the armchair again and took her on to his lap. 'That settles it, Elizabeth,' he said, 'you shall put me off no longer – we must be married right away. I know you have lived here for the last two years since your dear mother passed away and you have managed very well, but enough's enough. Poor love, you are frightened out of your wits – you need me to look after you.' *And I need your money*, he thought.

In the cottage Elizabeth put on one side the misgivings that had made her reluctant to accept his offer, agreed weakly and snuggled up to him for comfort.

In the graveyard the bones lay quiet now. Harriet had made the supreme effort and did not know that she had been neither understood nor heeded; nor did she know that if Elizabeth had not been frightened by seeing a ghastly apparition that night she would not have agreed to marry the man who was eventually to kill her and swing for it.

MY DEAR WIFE

R. CHETWYND-HAYES

Georgina looked even more beautiful than usual and very young, a fact that reminded Henry that his body, if not his soul, had long since left the sunlit meadows of youth, and was now walking along the shady avenues of middle age. One long-fingered white hand rested on his left arm and she radiated that air of 'I belong to you' that so irritated him.

'Will it be a large party?' she asked.

'About two dozen or so people, I should imagine. We won't stay long.'

Georgina pouted her lips. 'Oh, why not! It's such a long time since we went to a party. Let's stay until they throw us out.'

He tried to laugh. 'You may not like it. Remember the last one?'

'Please don't spoil things. I promise to be good.'

'Mind you are.'

They came at last to the large house that was one of a row in a long street. All the windows were lit up.

Godfrey Manning looked like a well-fed monkey that had been crammed into a faultlessly-tailored dinner jacket. He put an arm round Henry's shoulders and creased his face into a smile.

'So, you've come out of hiding, Henry! No one has seen you for simply ages.'

Henry twitched his left shoulder but the fat hand tightened its grip.

'I don't get out and about much these days. Anyone here that I know?'

At last the hand slid from his shoulders as Manning shrugged and looked listlessly round the room.

'There's the Websters – over there by the fireplace – dreadful bores. Simply oozing with middle-class respectability and late-night cocoa. Then there's that Nightingale creature. All boobs and bum.'

Henry took a tentative step to his right.

'Well, I'll have a mooch round. Don't worry about me.'

Manning's smile disappeared like a smear suddenly wiped from a window pane.

'Please yourself. There's a running buffet and plenty of booze.'

As Henry edged his way through the crowd he became aware that Georgina was watching him from the doorway, a tiny smile parting her lips; and that burning need to torment her, to watch her eyes become bright with unshed tears, sprang into irresistible life. He walked slowly towards the girl with blonde hair, taking careful note of the round face, the full lips, the languorous eyes, and knew that here was an easy conquest.

'My name,' he said quietly, 'is Henry Parkington.'

She giggled and Henry suddenly felt old and extremely bored and only the knowledge that Georgina was still watching him from the doorway kept the false smile on his face and the appreciative gleam in his eyes.

The girl murmured: 'Hallo, Henry Parkington. I'm Sheila Mayfield.'

Before he could answer, taped music blared from two wall amplifiers and Godfrey shouted: 'Dance, everybody. That's the way to get acquainted. Dance.'

Henry said: 'Shall we?' and they were soon swaying round the room, her head on his shoulder, their bodies pressed tight together. When they passed Georgina, Henry winked at her and experienced a thrill of guilty joy when he saw the white, drawn face and the pain-filled eyes. Then Godfrey turned out the lights and darkness erased the face, turned the room into a small blind world, where feminine voices squealed and bodies bumped one into the other. Henry heard Sheila gasp and shout: 'Stop it. You're hurting me.'

'What's the matter?' he asked, silently cursing Godfrey's infantile sense of humour.

'Someone is hitting me on the back.'

Henry raised his voice.

'Godfrey, for God's sake turn on the lights.'

There were cries of 'Spoilsport!' 'What's the matter, won't she play ball?' and other like pleasantries, but presently light exploded, killing the darkness with one searing flash, and he was staring down into Sheila's white, angry face. When she spoke her voice had lost its husky, seductive quality and was shrill, tinged with a slight northern accent.

'Some bleeder was hitting me in the back. Punching me.'

Henry looked angrily round the room and was just in time to see Georgina disappear through the doorway which led into the hall. Godfrey pushed his way through the crowd.

'Punching you, dear! My word – fancy that!'

'It was a woman,' Sheila added. 'With a cold, small fist.'

Godfrey bared his teeth in a simian grimace. 'Now which of you little darlings has been putting in the fist for old Henry. I know he's sweet – but a punch in the dark – really!'

'Someone pushed by me in the dark,' a man with a mauve face volunteered.

'Give her a drink and forget it,' a girl in a backless dress said. 'Worse things have happened in the dark.'

This remark brought a chorus of agreement and several young women began to recount experiences that ranged from the bizarre to the improbable. Henry led Sheila over to the wine table and poured her a generous helping of neat whisky.

'I should have known better than to come to one of Godfrey's parties,' she stated, having emptied the glass and held it out for replenishment. 'I mean to say – look at him!'

'Thank you, but I'd rather not,' Henry murmured.

Sheila sipped from her glass then reassumed her seductive mask.

'Have you got a car?'

Henry shook his head. 'I fear not. Me and a car – that's Britain's secret weapon.'

Sheila frowned. 'Now that's a great pity. I'm looking for a man with a car. I mean to say, you can go places in a car.'

'We could take a taxi,' Henry suggested, casting a quick glance at the hall doorway.

'We could, couldn't we? Say, that's an idea. This is a lousy party anyway.'

'But,' Henry added, taking one step towards the doorway, 'I must ask you to excuse me for a minute.'

'What? Oh, yeah – I get it. Don't be long.'

'No more than one minute – I promise. Tell you what. Why don't you phone for a taxi? The phone is over there in the window bay.'

She giggled. 'I'll do that. Yes, sir, I'll telephone for an old taxi.'

Henry found Georgina leaning against the wall by the front door. She was crying without sound, the tears glistening on her pale cheeks like diamonds on a slab of alabaster. Henry stood before her, his soul basking in the sun of righteous rage.

'You stupid, jealous bitch!'

'Please forgive me. But when I saw you making up to that – that creature, I just couldn't help myself.'

'You're mad. Raving mad.'

'Please don't be angry with me. I can't stand it when you're angry with me.'

Henry spat out the words, making each syllable a barbed dart.

'Get off my back. Do you hear me? I never want to see you again.'

He ignored her wail of anguish and went back into the crowded room. Sheila was standing by the wine table. Her eyes reminded him of a fire waiting for a scuttle of coal.

Sheila liked the lounge, admired the dining-room and gave her unstinted approval to the bedroom.

'The built-in wardrobes are so compact,' she murmured, 'and the bed so roomy. Know what I mean?'

'Perfectly,' Henry replied. 'Have a drink.'

'Just a teeny one. Too much moisture puts out the fire. Don't you agree?'

'Yes. But on the other hand a liberal application of paraffin will make it burn brighter.'

Her persistent giggle was becoming a little tiresome, but Henry told himself that one did not judge a saucepan by its rattle.

'You are clever,' she told him. 'Dishy and clever.'

'I have many virtues,' he agreed. 'Now where do we start?'

A scantily clad parcel is easy to unwrap, particularly when its contents have been crammed into a restricted space. Henry's practised hands completed their alloted task in just under two minutes and that which had been partially hidden was fully revealed. Then he looked up and saw Georgina's reflection in the mantelpiece mirror.

'Aren't we going into the bedroom?' Sheila asked.

Henry grinned as the reflected head turned away.

'I guess not, my angel. By now it will be occupied.'

Sheila sat up and looked anxiously at the open doorway.

'Occupied! But there's no one there.'

Henry leaned over and closed her mouth with a kiss.

'No one that need bother you.'

Only he heard the low sobbing that came from the bedroom, and presently, when lust had been sated, he felt the cold fingers of remorse gently caress his brain.

'But it's late,' Sheila protested. 'I'll never get a taxi at this time of night.'

'But you can't stay here,' Henry insisted.

'Why not?'

'Because my wife wouldn't like it.'

The girl stared at him with wide open mouth and glazed eyes.

'Your wife! You never mentioned you had a wife!'

'I didn't mention I had a goldfish, but there's one in the bowl over there.'

'You mean – your wife may come back at any moment?'

Henry sighed deeply as he realized that the sobbing cries had ceased some time ago.

'I mean she has been here for some little time, although she may have gone out again. She usually does when I have one of these lapses.'

For a short while silence reigned in the luxuriously appointed room, then Sheila poured out her rage.

'You dirty rotten bastard!'

'Last time this happened,' Henry went on, 'she went out and did not return for two entire days. But she did come back. She always does.'

'You filthy conceited pig.'

Henry looked at her dispassionately for a few seconds, then he sighed again.

'As you'll come back. You don't think so now, but later – nothing will keep you away.'

She stood up, then grabbed her handbag.

'You make me feel – soiled. Distinctly soiled. As though I hadn't washed for a thousand years.'

'Some men,' Henry remarked sadly, 'can't keep their women. Others can't lose them. It's nothing to do with looks, charm, sex appeal or any of the obvious things. No, it's indifference that gets you females going. When you realize a man doesn't give a damn if you live or die, you'll cut your throats to attract his attention.'

'I'm more likely to cut yours,' Sheila said, with – at that moment – deep sincerity.

'I should leave now,' Henry suggested softly. 'She may still be here and I'm in no mood for any more violence. One punch-up is sufficient for one night.'

He waited until the door had slammed, then got up and went into the bedroom. It was empty.

Henry became distinctly worried when, after a lapse of four days, Georgina had not put in an appearance. She had never been away for such a long time before and he wondered where she had gone. Was she walking along shadow-dressed streets, looking for the bright-tinted spectre of happiness? Or standing on a wild moor watching the white horse of hope perpetually galloping towards a limitless horizon?

Henry sent out winged thoughts that carried his appeal along the intricate network of communication channels that link all intelligent beings to the infinite.

'Come back to me. I want you back.'

On the fifth day Sheila came back.

'I have only come back for one reason,' Sheila said, 'and that is to tell you that I have no time for conceited, ill-mannered, heartless bastards who think they are God's gift to women.'

Henry nodded his full approval.

'I always value an honestly expressed opinion.'

'Furthermore,' Sheila continued, 'I wanted to make one point absolutely clear. I hate you more than I've ever hated any man in my entire life.'

'Hate is the childhood of love.'

She sat down on the sofa beside him and drew one finger gently down his left cheek.

'You know what I'd like to do?'

'No.'

'Carve deep scars down your face so that no woman would want to look at you again.'

'But they would. Women can never resist the grotesque.'

For a while neither spoke, then Sheila asked:

'Did she come back?'

He shook his head. 'No. She did not come back.'

Presently Sheila began to cry. She cried without tears, harsh body-shaking sobs that all but smothered the grief-tortured words.

'I'm so ashamed. I . . . I loathe myself. Loathe.'

As Henry gathered her into his arms he could not resist the thought that there should be violins playing in the background.

'I suppose,' he said after a while, 'I'd better carry you into the bedroom. It's considered good manners.'

Sheila smothered her sighs and replaced them with a giggle.

'Don't bother. I'll run.'

On the sixth day Georgina came back.

The shrill voice went echoing down the corridors of Henry's brain and made him think longingly of the cool cloisters of a monastery that had never been desecrated by a woman's foot.

'You bloody, bent swine! How could you do this to me?'

He came up on to one elbow and eyed her naked form with the detachment that belongs to a gourmet after a long and satisfying feast.

'What have I done now?'

Sheila glared at him, then shot a rather fearful glance at the doorway.

'You know damn well what I mean. Your wife – she's back.'

Henry sat upright. 'Are you sure?'

'Of course I'm bloody sure. She was standing in the doorway watching us. The damned black-haired bitch.'

Henry slid off the bed and slid into a dressing-gown.

'Well, that being the case I'd better have a word with her. Will you excuse me for a moment?'

'Excuse you! Look, this isn't just someone who's turned up unexpectedly at a tea party.'

'Are you absolutely certain you saw her?'

For a moment it seemed as if Sheila had lost the power of speech, then she quickly corrected this assumption.

'I saw a black-haired, large-eyed woman, with a white face that was long as next week, standing in the doorway. Was that your wife or some other poor bitch you have been stringing along?'

'What was she wearing?' Henry asked.

'A long white evening dress.'

Henry nodded. 'That was Georgina. Funny.'

'I'm glad you think so.'

Henry went out into the passage and made his way into the lounge.

Georgina was sitting in an armchair that was situated to the right of the fireplace and Henry thought she had never looked so sad. He sank down before her and peered up into her eyes.

'Is there any point in saying I'm sorry?'

This was a question he had asked often in the past; arranging the words a little differently in the beginning, but always knowing she would allow optimism to triumph over experience. Now he was forced to consider the possibility that the well of forgiveness had run dry.

'I will send her away. If you will stay with me I will never . . . never . . . look at another woman again. I promise I will be for all time a better man.'

A solitary tear ran down from Georgina's left eye, then fell upon the bosom of her white dress. Her voice came whispering down the road that is paved with dead years.

'I don't want a better man. Oh, merciful God, I don't want a better man.'

'I will send her away,' he repeated. 'I will never look at another woman again.'

Sheila wept.

She did more. She screamed, kicked, clung to doorposts, pronounced words that are not usually listed in a young lady's vocabulary, and loudly proclaimed her intention of mounting a perpetual guard in the corridor.

'She's not taking back what's mine. I've paid for you with

shame, self-respect and five days of pure hell.'

'Go away,' Henry advised, detaching one hand from the doorpost, 'and have a little think. Remember you are young and beautiful, I'm nothing to write home about and this entire business is bloody silly.'

He finally got her into the corridor, then, as an added precaution, pushed her into a lift and did not move until the doors had closed and hidden his latest sin.

Presently Georgina came out from the flat and joined him.

The days that followed a making-up were always eventful. Georgina did not leave Henry for longer than fifteen minutes at one time and followed him almost everywhere. Buses, trains, office, church – he once went there to pray – there was never an opportunity to complain of loneliness. When he went to his tailor, Georgina sat on a straight-backed chair and shook her head at the pin-striped material which Henry – up to that moment – had considered rather becoming. She whispered 'Horrid', when the shoemaker produced the made-to-measure light tan brogues; and said: 'Really, darling!' when faced with the yellow capped, thick-soled slip-ons.

Henry realized that this was loving criticism; an expression of the deep regard Georgina had for his welfare, and it would be an act of black ingratitude if he were to display the slightest sign of irritation. Instead he smiled indulgently and promised only to wear the offending articles when his Aunt Matilda paid a visit – a personage whom Georgina had never liked.

For three weeks Henry walked the straight path of the newly converted. Curvaceous blondes with come-hither eyes were ignored. Invitations to temptation-ridden parties were torn into very small pieces. Telephone calls from Sheila were terminated the moment she uttered a single word.

But Georgina was cursed with an appetite that gobbled up happiness and demanded constant and ever larger helpings.

'Let us,' she said with deceptive calmness, 'stock up the fridge, cut off the telephone, burn all correspondence and create a small world of our own.'

'But I must go out sometimes,' Henry pleaded, 'otherwise people will think I'm dead.'

'What does that matter?' she insisted. 'After all – they think I'm dead.'

'Well . . .' He paused, knowing from experience that this subject was a dangerous one and could lead to complicated arguments. 'Well . . . aren't you?'

As was to be expected, Georgina began to cry and again there was the urge to torment her, rub the salt of truth into raw wounds. He raised his voice.

'Look, it's no use kidding yourself. You are dead. D.E.A.D. Dead . . . dead. Remember?'

'Please . . . please don't . . .'

'Let's stop pussy-footing about and face facts. Your damn jealousy made both of our lives pure hell and you finally . . .'

'How can you be so cruel?'

'. . . hanged yourself from a beam in the attic . . .'

'I'm not going to listen. When you behave like this I don't know you. How can you love me and still say such dreadful things?'

Henry pulled up a chair and sat facing his dear – dear wife. The mask of pretence slipped and for the first time in five years he deliberately looked directly into the awful face of reality.

'It was at that party. Remember? The one given by the Fortesques. I flirted a little . . .'

'You tortured me. You knew I was half mad with jealousy. You knew.'

'I only knew you put on a face like a wet weekend whenever I looked at another woman. Then you bought a length of clothesline and hanged yourself. OK. So you decided to call it a day. It was your life. But for God's sake – why hang on?'

For a second – a minute – an eternity – Georgina looked at him, then, after parting her lips with a pale ghost of a smile, said:

'Because you won't let me go.'

'That's damn stupid.'

Georgina lowered her voice and spoke in that lilting whisper he could never forget.

'Your love is a double-edged sword. It killed me and your peace of mind – both at the same time. When I am here you torture me – when I go away and the lamp of memory dims –

you call me back. So it will be until the end of time. Every man creates his own hell.'

His head jerked up and anger – fear – coated his words with venom.

'The house of death must be lined with platitudes.'

'I am only a voice that echoes along the halls of your brain.'

The door chimes pealed their familiar tune and Henry found himself silently repeating the old nursery rhyme, but it was Georgina who sang the words.

'"You owe me five farthings, say the bells of St Martin's."'

Henry did not move and presently Georgina asked:

'Aren't you going to let her in?'

'Never. I promised.'

'You have promised so many times before.'

The chimes spoke again.

'"When will you pay me? say the bells of Old Bailey."'

Henry stood up and shouted: 'Go away. I never want to see you again. Can't you get that through your stupid head? I don't want to see either of you again.'

Georgina's white hand flew to her mouth and she took one step backwards.

'You don't mean that. You can't.'

He sat down and shook his head.

'At this moment I don't know what I mean.'

'Perhaps,' Georgina suggested softly, 'you want both of us.'

The central-heating boiler was a well-behaved piece of equipment and therefore required little attention. When the hall porter entered the small underground room and turned on the light, his eyes went first to the large dial which registered the amount of oil that still remained in the tank, then – with a sudden jerk of head – took due note of what was hanging from an overhead beam. He said: 'Strewth!' followed by: 'Gawd, help us!' then, having for the time being run out of words, was violently sick. Later he strengthened his soul, quelled his rebellious stomach and went forth to proclaim the news that Sheila had hanged herself with a length of wire flex.

Clara was a petite brunette who was well endowed with everything but brains. She looked up over Henry's right shoulder and exclaimed: 'Oh, my!'

Henry sighed. He often did these days. 'What's wrong now?'

Clara nodded in the direction of the open doorway.

'Them. I do think it is very naughty of you to let those awful creatures watch. I really do.'

Henry rose up and smiled sardonically. 'Yes, it's funny the way some people get their kicks. You would think that they would know when they're not wanted.'

The long, white faces of Georgina and Sheila were wet with tears, as they turned away and went out to walk shadow-dressed streets, for ever doomed to seek the swift-footed spectre of happiness. Presently Henry, replete, but suffering from remorseful indigestion, would call them back. In the meanwhile Clara sobbed, shed beautiful crystal-clear tears and announced her irrevocable, unshakable decision.

'I am going away and I will never – never – not even if you get down on your bended knees – come back.'

Henry groaned. 'You will. By the great Lord Lucifer and all his angels – you will.'

She did.